ALSO BY **Jody. J. Little**
Mostly the Honest Truth

Jody J. Little

HARPER
An Imprint of HarperCollinsPublishers

Library of Congress Control Number: 2019944932
ISBN 978-0-06-285258-8

Typography by Jenna Stempel-Lobell
20 21 22 23 24   PC/LSCH   10 9 8 7 6 5 4 3 2 1
❖
First Edition

For my entire family—
may you all embrace your "weird."
But especially for Steve, Alli, and Ryan,
I love you.

Chapter One

A Summer Plan

On the second-to-last day of sixth grade, I wake up to my parents snoring on the futon couch across the living room.

They snore in perfect rhythm.

It's like a timed loop in a computer program, really.

Hank gargles on the inhale.

Coral whistles on the exhale.

Repeat.

In a tiny house like ours, I don't get my own room like most twelve-year-olds. I get a corner, with a twin-size futon, unfolded on the floor. It's my island, 39 by 75 inches of space just for me.

But today, I don't mind seeing Hank and Coral across the room, because if they are sleeping on the living room futon, then our cousin James is sleeping in their bedroom.

He's here.

Finally.

My very first thought is to spring off my island and rush to the bedroom to wake him up. I have so much to tell him, and so many questions to ask. But then I remember my plan, and I hold my eagerness in because a plan is like a computer program. You don't jump ahead and leave out steps. Missing steps means one thing is certain: ERROR.

My school-issued laptop is in its spot under my pillow. I slide it out and cover myself with blankets. This is my last morning with this beautiful device. All computers and equipment must be returned today to our tech teacher, Mrs. Naberhaus. Linking on to our neighbor's Wi-Fi, I open our class blog one last time. I skim the posts about upcoming summer vacations, clicking Like as I go. Pilar is going to Hawaii. Austin is hiking in the gorge for seven days. Aditi is visiting her grandparents in India. I wish I could share my summer plans too, but I can't. Not yet. Not until I talk to James.

I navigate to my emails and tap to open the message from Mrs. Naberhaus, from two weeks ago.

Hi Mac,
See the attached flyer. I think this opportunity is perfect for you. The instructor's a friend of mine. With her guidance in an intensive camp like this, your coding skills will soar. I hope you'll talk to your parents.
Sincerely, Mrs. Naberhaus

Clicking open the attachment, I read it for the thousandth time.

Summer Coding Camp

Learn Python and C++ to create a new app or game

For incoming 7th graders only

Eight-week session begins June 28

Every day, Monday through Friday 9 a.m. to 3 p.m.

All materials and devices are provided. Bring your own lunch.

Cost: $500

This is it, my summer plan.

I haven't talked to Hank and Coral because I know they'll say no. But James is here now, and who can better convince my parents that I should attend a computer camp than the chief information officer of Technobotical Software?

That's my hope, anyway. I cross my fingers and squeeze them tight.

"Mac?"

Peeking out from under my blankets, I see Hank. He's shielding his eyes from the electron beams shooting out of my screen.

"Could you close that? It throws my morning energies out of alignment."

"Sorry." I shut the laptop and tuck it into my schoolbag, along with my notebooks and binder.

"Are you going out to feed the chickens?" Hank asks.

I'm not sure why he's asking, since feeding the chickens and collecting their eggs is my morning chore. I shrug the question aside and scoot off my island, folding and tucking the ends of my sheets and blankets around my futon. Then I select a pair of jeans and a clean T-shirt from the cattail basket that serves as my dresser and walk the eleven steps to the bathroom to dress in private. I comb my long brown hair, separate it into three equal parts, and weave it into a tight braid down my back.

Tiptoeing out of the bathroom, I grab Coral's hemp-fiber egg basket from the hook in the kitchen and slink outside to the garage, which is not really a garage at all since Hank converted it to a chicken coop. There's 144 by 240 inches of private living space for his flock of three. Nine futon islands could fit in here with space left over. I've done the calculations.

Livie, Divie, and Bolivie, the White Leghorn poultry triplets, strut around the straw-lined garage floor. They ignore me completely and jerk themselves out the opened door toward the lawn, ready to peck for whatever it is that free-range chickens peck for.

I check the water bucket and the feeder, and add more grains, but as I move toward their nesting boxes to collect the three fresh eggs, I hear a soft clucking.

There, perching on a roost, is another chicken.

"Who are you?" I ask, which is a ridiculous question to pose to a nearly brainless animal.

I step back to check out this strange fowl. She's not a White Leghorn. Deep red and brown feathers cover her rather skinny body. Her head is crooked, like someone bent her neck to the right and it stuck there.

"Hey! Shoo!" I wave my hands toward the garage door.

She doesn't budge. She just sits on the perch and twitches her crooked head.

I reach for an egg, keeping my eye on the strange hen. She keeps clucking, looking at me with glazed eyes.

"You don't belong here."

And then, just as I stand up straight, the squatting fowl launches herself off the roost, right toward my face. Her wings flap twice, swatting me in the forehead.

"Ahhhh!" My arms flail in the air, spinning the basket upside down. The egg inside lands on the garage floor, splatting on the cement.

"Look what you did!"

I wipe at my forehead to check for blood, then grab a pair of Coral's gardening gloves so I can scoop up the slimy egg mess and drop it in the compost. Gathering the remaining eggs, I storm back into the house to report the lost egg and the unwanted intruder.

Coral is up, chopping her garden kale and collards, when I enter the kitchen. My forehead stings from the nasty bird's wing lashing.

"Thank you, MacKenna." She kisses my cheek. Her blond dreadlocks tickle my face, and a new trinket twisted into one of her dreads taps me in the eye. Coral collects discarded plastic bits and stores them in her hair. She considers it her way of protesting the devastation of Mother Earth by the horrors of plastic.

Coral is the only person who calls me by my full first name. Actually, I have three Mac names, MacKenna MacKensie MacLeod, but three Macs is excessive. It doesn't adhere to the coding principle of D.R.Y., which stands for *Don't repeat yourself.* The triple Mac is like having unnecessary steps, so I prefer just Mac.

As for Hank and Coral, I've never called them Dad and Mom.

Hank and Coral don't like titles.

"A stray chicken got into the garage," I say. "Hank needs to find out where it came from and get it out."

Hank saunters into the kitchen now, yawning, tugging on his rust-colored beard, which hangs to his midchest. "So, you met Poppy."

"Poppy?"

"Isn't she a beauty?" Hank gushes. "She's a Rhode Island Red, an excellent breed for urban coops."

"She's yours?"

"She is now." Hank reaches into the cupboard for his favorite green tea mug.

"But . . . but you can't keep her. The city of Portland chicken ordinance clearly states that you can only keep three or fewer chickens on your property unless you get a permit."

Hank laughs. "Oh, I don't think I need a permit, Mac."

"Yes, you do. Those are the rules. You could get a citation."

Why did I always have to explain things like this to my parents?

"I'm not worried about a citation."

But I am.

I'm forever worried when it comes to Hank and Coral.

I slump into a chair at the kitchen table. "Is my forehead red or scratched?" I point right under my hairline.

Coral comes over to investigate. "You do have a scratch, honey. What happened?"

"That illegal chicken attacked me."

"The poor thing," Hank says. "She must be distressed. I'll get my drum out later this afternoon. Maybe that will calm her."

It's not lost on me that Hank appears more concerned with this new chicken than he is for me and my injury.

I sigh and reach for one of the unsweetened carrot

muffins on the table and take a bite, chewing for the sake of sustenance only. I long to teleport to Willa's kitchen, where her mom's probably making pancakes with syrup and bacon. Or to Brie's kitchen, where she's likely eating a steaming bowl of her father's pho.

"Two days of school left, MacKenna. Seventh grade is just around the corner." Coral sits down at the table across from me. "Are you as stoked about summer as we are?"

For the first time ever, I *am* stoked about summer.

Because this summer is going to be different, thanks to my plan. It won't be the usual ten excruciating weeks with Hank and Coral, where I spend my days with chickens and garden compost, and help make natural fiber baskets and soap, and wipe down yoga mats with vinegar solutions.

And the best part of my summer plan is that I will not have to deal with Hank and Coral's week-long Mother Earth Festival, an endless seven days of smelly, long-haired, barefoot people, drumming and dancing and singing. They used to all camp in the yard, but the cops came by two summers ago after a neighbor complained about the tents. Hank and Coral were slapped with citations for illegal city camping, so now all the strangers sleep inside, in the living room, surrounding my futon island.

"Wait until you hear what Hank has planned for the festival." Coral beams.

Oh, I can wait.

I can wait a long time.

Before Coral begins to share the plans, a hairy-chested, bearded man wearing nothing but soccer shorts ambles into the kitchen.

I blink about fifty times trying to focus on this man in front of me. "James?" My voice is shaky and uncertain. Is this really him?

Coral rises and takes the man's wrist. She squeezes his hand and bounces up and down on her toes, like she's a child holding the hand of Santa Claus. "MacKenna, James now wants to be called Coho."

"Co . . . Coho?"

Did I hear that right? Isn't Coho a salmon? Why is the CIO of Technobotical Software going by the name of a fish?

"Hey, Mac. It's been a while," the man named Coho, formerly known as our cousin James, says. He moves toward me like he wants to hug me, but I quickly extend my hand and he shakes it instead.

"Coho brought us Poppy," Hanks announces.

"Who we need a permit for," I remind them. But inside my mind, I'm not really thinking about a rogue chicken. Other, more important questions are firing around, like what happened to James? Why does he look like . . . like Hank? Where are his pressed khaki pants and white button-up shirt and polished penny loafers?

Coral drops James's—Coho's—hand and puts her arm

9

around my shoulders. "MacKenna, Coho is exploring new paths, and this new energy inside him is colossal. Can't you just feel it?"

"No." I thought his old energy was colossal, his energy of codes and numbers and sequences, and brilliantly engineered devices. The energy that filled me with hope for my future as a computer programmer, far, far away from chickens and drums and stale sugarless carrot muffins.

"I have to get to school." I rise from the kitchen chair, feeling a little queasy.

"Let's talk later, Mac," Coho says, but I don't respond. I just bob my head in agreement.

"Wait, MacKenna. Do you mind if I borrow your bicycle today? I'm going to loan mine to Coho. It'll fit him better." Coral beams at me. "We're going to meet up with some bicycling friends this afternoon for a few photos."

I shrug. "Sure, I guess, but . . ." I eye Coral and the man I used to call James. "You're not going to do something weird with my bike, are you? I don't want any adjustments or bells and whistles added."

Coral laughs. "I'm just going to be riding it, sweetheart. I promise."

Coho laughs too and scratches his beard.

I feel my summer plan begin to crumble beneath me.

Chapter Two

Hippie Chicken

Without my bike, I race the twenty blocks to school to get there on time. Thoughts and questions blend inside me the whole way. What's going on with our cousin? What are these paths he's exploring? Will he still help me convince Hank and Coral that this coding camp is important?

I enter the front door of Winterhill Middle School, panting down the main hallway toward my classroom, barely focusing. I feel someone jostle me on the side, but I keep moving. Austin passes me, flapping his arms. "Hey, Hippie Chick-chick-chicken, you got feathers in your hair."

The insult wakes me up. I glare at him.

Hippie Chicken.

I've been called names since the first day of first grade when our teacher, Mrs. Grubb, asked us to draw a picture of something we did over the summer. I drew our Earth Festival, with people sitting on grass in a circle with bongo drums in their laps. I added little music symbols to show them singing and thumping on their drums. I drew our chickens too. On the lines below my picture I tried my first-grade best at writing a sentence. *We had a sumer festvl.*

When everyone finished their drawings, Mrs. Grubb told us to come to the carpet at the front of the room and share, one at a time.

Brie went to Disneyland with her family and saw Mickey Mouse. She drew spinning teacups and the Matterhorn roller coaster. "It's the happiest place on earth!" she said.

I'd never been to Disneyland.

Austin went to the coast. His picture had sand and waves. "I made a giant sandcastle!" he said.

I'd never been to the coast. I'd only made castles in Coral's garden compost.

Willa drew a picture of her birthday party with balloons, a big pink frosted cake, and lots of presents wrapped in colorful paper. "I got ballet slippers."

I had birthday parties with Hank and Coral's friends. They wrapped my gifts in towels.

When it was my turn, I held up my picture of the drums and the music notes.

"What's this, Mac?" Mrs. Grubb asked.

"Our summer Earth Festival."

Mrs. Grubb's eyebrows lifted.

"Every summer people come to our house for bongo

drumming and dancing, and we make crafts."

"Why, that's a unique tradition," my teacher said.

Austin and the other boys began to giggle. He pointed at my picture. "Bongo Girl." Then he snickered some more. I felt like a stinkbug. Maybe I smelled like one too.

"Boys," Mrs. Grubb said, "be polite. It's Mac's turn. Mac, do you have more to share?"

I shook my head. I was done sharing. I didn't want to be Bongo Girl. I wanted to be a girl with a pink cake. I wanted to be a girl who flew to Disneyland. I still want that.

I snap out of my bad memory daydream and scowl at Austin, but when I smooth my braid, three small reddish feathers drift to the floor.

Poppy feathers.

He laughs some more. *"Bawk-bawk-bawk!"* he squawks as he walks away.

I turn around to scoop up the feathers, but when I do I find myself nearly nose to nose with someone else. The someone brushes his straggly black bangs from his eyes with one hand and extends his other hand toward me to reveal the Poppy feathers.

Joey Marino.

He's new this year. I've never even spoken to him, yet here he is helping me. I take the feathers from his open palm. "Thank . . ."

"MAC!"

I jerk quickly to see Willa grand jeté-ing toward me, her blond curls springing up and down like coils. Brie glides along next to her like the athletic half dolphin she is. They link arms with me.

Willa Moore and Brie Vo.

If it weren't for the two of them, I'd be permanently positioned as a middle school bottom-feeder, clinging to the lowest rung on my classmates' hierarchy ladder, a forever stinkbug. But Willa had looped her elbow with mine not long after the first-grade sharing episode. She'd leaned toward me and said, "Brie and I like dancing and drums. We'd come to the Earth Festival." They are the only two people at school who don't call me names, laugh at my clothes, or tease me about my parents.

I turn back around to finish thanking Joey, but he's gone. "Did you guys see where he went?"

"Who?" Willa says.

"Joey Marino."

"The new kid?" Willa asks.

Brie spins around. "I don't see him. Why?"

I turn in every direction, looking for the gray T-shirt, dark jeans, and scuffed black combat boots he wears every day. I might be the only person who notices that. Maybe it's because my secondhand wardrobe is similarly limited.

Garage-Sale Girl. Mac and Trash.

"He's kind of a phantom, don't you think?" Willa asks.

She's right. Joey Marino has a way of appearing out of the blue, like a magician waved his wand and pulled him out of a hat. Ta-da!

And he disappears just as quickly. Poof!

"What are the feathers for, Mac?" Brie asks.

"New chicken." I toss them in the hallway garbage bin just as the bell rings.

Willa grabs my arm. "Come on, Mac. Let's dance to class. There's only two days of school left."

Brie strides forward, leading the way. Willa chassés with pointed toes, holding one of my hands, and I touch my head, smoothing my braid, checking for more stray feathers.

I barely listen to Mr. Miller talk about the summer reading list. I watch the second hand of the clock tick, tick. I borrow Willa's plastic sharpener and place my pencil in the hole, twisting it slowly, studying how the shaved-off piece forms a perfect spiral. I doodle spirals on the margins of a paper, and my brain automatically figures out the nested loops I would use to code them. I have to talk to . . . Coho about this coding camp. I need his help convincing Hank and Coral.

When I write a computer code, I can block out the weirdness of their world. No one tells me to consider the size of my carbon footprint. When I code, no one tells me my pants are muddy, *Skunk Stripe*, or that I have chicken feed on my shirt, *Little Red Hen*. No one sneers at the kale and kohlrabi chips in my lunch, *Kalebrains*. When I code no one . . .

"Mac. Mac!" Willa leans down. Her nose is practically touching mine.

"What?"

"It's time for tech class. Why are you drawing snails?"

I just shake my head and quickly put my supplies away.

Tech class breezes by as always, and with ten minutes left in the period, Mrs. Naberhaus tells us to line up and turn in our laptops for the summer. I go to the end of the line. I want to hold this computer for as long as I possibly can.

When I get to her desk, she smiles. "Mac, did you talk to your parents about the camp?"

I nod, but I'm lying. I don't mention that I'm still working through my plan.

"I have something for you," she says. "Set your laptop on that pile."

She pulls down the poster that hung behind her desk all year. *Girls Are Supercoders*. She hands it to me. "You should have this. Coding is *your* superpower."

Every neuron in my body flickers with life. I wish she would tell Hank and Coral this. "Thank you."

"I still don't have your application form. Do you need another one?"

I lie again and nod my head yes. The form is in my binder. Blank. Waiting for approval.

Mrs. Naberhaus shuffles through the papers on her desk. "I checked this morning and there are only two slots in the camp left. Get it back to me quickly with that five-hundred-dollar payment too." She hands me another application.

All those livened neurons go dead.

There are so many obstacles.

Two slots left.

Five hundred dollars.

Parents who believe technology is destroying the earth.

But I still have hope. There's still Coho. He may have changed his name and grown a beard, but he's still the same inside.

Isn't he?

I roll up the poster and tuck it under my arm.

Girls Are Supercoders.

Chapter Three

The Sighting at the Joan of Arc Statue

After school, Willa, Brie, and I take a long walk, killing some time before Brie has swim practice.

We're walking side by side on Glisan Street when Willa hoists herself onto the brick wall around a neighborhood church. She raises her arms and shrieks, "One more day of school!"

"Willa! Get down. You're so loud," Brie says.

"You guys, it's almost summer. Come up here with me." Willa wiggles her skinny hips, hollering, "No more sixth grade!"

"Don't fall," Brie says, but she's laughing, and she effortlessly lifts her body onto the wall and stands by Willa.

"My soul needs to dance," Willa says. "You should both try it."

"My parents seem to think my soul needs to swim." Brie

waves her arms in a breaststroke motion. "That's my whole summer, training for the state meet in August."

"Chlorination time," Willa sings, mimicking Brie's arm motions.

"It never ends."

"Mac, get up here. You're missing all the fun." Willa pumps her palms in the air.

I walk back to the lowest part of the brick wall and step up, inching my way toward my friends.

Willa grabs my hand when I get to her and lifts it in the air. "What are your parents doing for their Earth Festival this year? Making drums? Making dream pillows?"

"I don't even want to know." I remember Coral's mention of some big plans this morning.

"You know, Willa, there's always dancing at Mac's Earth Festival. You should go," Brie suggests.

"It's not *my* festival." I feel dizzy from the height of the wall, so I sit down, dangling my feet over the bricks. "Besides, I'm not doing anything with their festival because I'm still planning to go to that computer camp."

"You mean your parents said yes?" Willa asks.

"Well, not—"

"You haven't asked them, have you?" Brie sits down next to me and bumps my shoulder.

In my head, I can hear Hank's response: *Mac, we feel*

there could be a negative impact on your internal spiritual growth if you sit in front of a screen all day.

And Coral's follow-up: *MacKenna, we believe your young eyes need to absorb and then reflect the beauty of the earth we live on.*

And then they would stare at me with distant, dreamy smiles, looking right through me, their daughter made of glass, seeing something on the other side of me that only they want to see.

Willa drops down on my other side, swinging her legs against the brick wall. "What about your cousin James? He's going to help you convince them, right?"

I'm halted from answering, because at that moment, there's a burst of *ting-ting-tings* and a sudden convergence of people and bicycles around the golden Joan of Arc statue in the middle of the Glisan Street roundabout.

And the people are . . .

"Oh my God!" I freeze.

Brie screams.

The people all line up in a row in front of Joan of Arc.

Willa bounces to her feet and roars in laughter. "The Portland Naked Bikers!"

Willa's right. Every person by the statue straddles their bikes in various forms of nudity. Some attempt to conceal their . . . parts . . . with body paint and glitter. Some wear thick leis around their necks and grass skirts around their waists.

And there, standing in the middle of the row of near nakedness, is Coral.

Her dreadlocks drape over her pale-skinned shoulders.

She wears some sort of leafy green bikini—her organic garden kale, perhaps.

Next to Coral stands Coho, our cousin, the CIO of Technobotical Software. He also wears something leafy below his naval.

Willa continues to laugh. "How long has your mom been a naked biker?" She slaps me on the shoulder with the back of her hand.

For a long, long time. It's something I've never told my friends. Some family secrets should remain deep, deep underground. I grip the brick wall with my fingers. Even sitting down, I feel like I might topple over.

Willa's still standing, gaping at the bikers. Brie has the decency to turn her back, but she's laughing too, the shock of the initial sighting now worn off.

Somehow, I manage to unfreeze myself, but I'm not laughing. I squeeze my eyes shut to hide the sight at the statue. I hope there are no cops. This isn't a planned, sanctioned naked biking event, is it? Isn't this indecent exposure in broad daylight? I'm certain there are city laws against this.

"Mac!" Willa slaps my shoulder again. "Is that your bike?"

My eyes pop open and squint at the mortifying sight before me.

Coral sits on *my* bicycle. My eighteen-speed mountain bike that I told her this morning she could borrow.

Coral is riding *my* bike *naked*!

Willa keeps laughing. She's close to tears. "I gotta get a photo!"

"No, you don't," I holler. "Stop looking at them!"

"Mac, this is hilarious."

"Willa, don't." Brie grabs Willa's phone.

I lean over, my hands on my knees, wheezing.

"You can't tell *anyone*." I seek my friends' faces, urging them to remain silent, imagining the horrifying names I might be called for this. *Bikebutt. Nudist Mama.*

Brie glares at Willa. "We aren't going to say anything, right, Willa?"

"Well, I won't say a word, but I don't know about him." She points across Glisan Street.

I follow Willa's finger, which aims directly at a boy on the corner across the street.

Joey Marino.

He raises his hand and waves at all three of us.

I hunch over and close my eyes again. I silently wish for

a crevasse to appear in the sidewalk so the wall I'm sitting on will collapse and I'll instantly fall inside the gap.

No. Backspace. Delete that.

I want a crevasse to appear around Coral, so *she* will fall inside . . . and Coho can go with her.

Just then, a new stab of panic hits my chest. What if Joey Marino says something? Does he know Coral is my mom? I should go talk to him. Make sure he . . .

But when I look up, he's not there.

He's vanished.

Again.

Chapter Four

Money

I arrive home to find Hank in the garage drumming for Poppy. Coral is home too. I see her through the kitchen window, standing at the sink. Fortunately, she now has a shirt on.

I avoid my parents and walk around the house to the front door. Inside, Coho sits crisscross on the futon couch, strumming a guitar and wailing a song about mountain air.

"Hey, Mac." He stops playing when I close the door. "Great to see you again."

I look at our cousin's scruffy beard, and the same soccer shorts he wore this morning, and the guitar on his lap. An enormous lump of air forms in my throat. He gazes at me. Maybe he can see the lump growing. Maybe he can read all the questions swirling in my brain.

"Sit, Mac." He scoots to the edge of the futon.

"Why did you change your name?" It seems like a good question to start with.

"It felt right. A new path needs a clean slate, a clearing away of old energies and titles."

"Are you on vacation?" I ask. "How long are you staying? Where's your car?"

"I quit my job, Mac."

"You what?"

"I was getting signals. Physical signals. I was feeling an internal resistance to my external daily life. Tingles. Rashes. Itching. Stomach pains. It was excruciating." Coho's face pales as he speaks.

"Are you sick?" I'm struggling to swallow the lump in my throat, but I keep trying.

"Not anymore. I took two weeks off. I escaped the city and unplugged. No electronics. Nothing. Just me, my thoughts, and the earth surrounding me."

These don't sound like the words James normally speaks. They sound like things Hank and Coral would say. I want him to pull out his three laptops and show me the programs he's written to increase the efficiency of the company's business reports.

I want to pull the forms for my coding camp out of my bag and show him the opportunity that awaits me. I want to unroll my poster, *Girls Are Supercoders*, and watch his face light up like it did two years ago when I showed him the school projects I made with the microcomputer, the weather station, the arcade stick.

But Coho just keeps speaking his new language. "Those two weeks made me evolve into a new human, Mac. The physical pain is gone. I feel I've reached an enlightened moment. The world of technology imprisoned me on a single path."

My hand moves to my throat. The lump has burst. Little bits and pieces of it flow through me. Some bits form twinges and tingles on my arms. Some pieces rush to my face, forming tears. I stand up and turn my back to Coho.

"I have surprises coming your way, Mac, but I'll give you some space now. We'll talk later." He touches my shoulder and heads to the kitchen.

Coho has surprised me enough already. I don't think I want to talk to him anymore. I don't need another Hank and Coral person in my life. I need someone on my side. Someone to help me.

I flop down on my futon island and stare at the blank wall. I can hear voices in the kitchen. I smell sandalwood from Coral's incense burner.

Sitting up, I pull the poster Mrs. Naberhaus gave me from my bag and I unroll it.

Girls Are Supercoders.

How will I go to this camp now? My entire plan is falling

apart. None of the original steps are working. I'll have to refactor it all.

Obstacle number one: I need a good story for Hank and Coral, explaining what I'm doing for the eight weeks of camp. It must be a perfectly sound, environmentally conscious reason to be away from home all day. Maybe I can tell them I'm pulling invasive ivy from the wetlands near the river. They'll love that.

Obstacle number two: I need to get the form signed with a parent signature.

Hmmm . . . my eyes scan the living room and pause at the bookshelf. There's a basket where Coral tosses papers, some to keep and some to recycle. Rising from my futon island, I sift through the papers and find what I'm looking for . . . Hank's scribble of a signature. I grab a pencil and attempt to copy it. My fifth attempt is pretty close.

This is forgery, and it's illegal.

But it's worth it to go to this camp.

Obstacle number three is my biggest: the five-hundred-dollar price tag. Without Coho's help, where will I get the money?

Inside a wooden box is my life savings, consisting of bills and coins I've found and collected. I don't even have to count it. I know how much I have: $29.33. That leaves me a balance of $470.67.

There must be a way to get money. And I'll figure it

out, just like I figure out the right commands for all my programming challenges.

I take out some paper and begin a flowchart. I title it *How to Get $500*. In a box at the top I write in $29.33, and then I add new boxes. One for walking our neighbor's dog once school ends. He'll pay me two dollars each morning walk. My brain quickly calculates the earnings . . . ten weeks of summer, seven days each week gives me $140. I fill that in the box. But I won't have $140 in time to pay for the camp. I scratch it out and write in $20.

I make a box for *Money Found*.

I make a box titled *Borrow from Willa?*

Another for *Borrow from Brie?*

I sketch in several more blank boxes for other income ideas.

If I received allowance, I could write that in, but Hank and Coral have always refused. "MacKenna, the family unit is a community," they say. "Everyone pitches in. Everyone is rewarded."

But I never feel rewarded. Willa gets twenty dollars a week to spend as she pleases. I'm not sure if she does any chores. Maybe laundry, but her parents have a washing machine. They don't hand-wash clothes in the sink with homemade organic soaps.

If I still had my school laptop, I could do a search right now: *Best way for a 12-year-old to earn money.*

Maybe I could sell something. I write *Sell Stuff* in one of the boxes on my flowchart. Maybe the chicken eggs. But four eggs a day wouldn't earn much, and Hank would notice.

What about Coral's scented candles? But who would buy them? And how many could I really sell?

Coral pops her head in the living room doorway and smiles. "MacKenna? Dinner's ready."

She's made kale salad. I stare at the chopped leaves of power greens, wondering if these leaves are fresh from the garden, or whether they were picked earlier in the morning and then worn. . . .

I put my fork down.

Hank touches my hand. "Mac, it looks like you're absorbing something intense right now."

"I am," I say truthfully. "I'm thinking about how to earn some money."

Coral laughs and says to Coho, "Our MacKenna's very attached to her financial future."

Coho nods. "And so was I, but, Mac"—he speaks softly—"money does not bring you the true serenity you need."

Coral nods back at him.

Coho continues: "The thing about money, Mac—"

"I'm sorry." I push my chair back. "May I be excused? I have a few things to do before the last day of school."

"Definitely," Hank says. "Go sort out your thoughts, Mac. I'll drum for you later."

I raise my palm. "No, I'm good. Really."

It's a lie, but drumming isn't going to help.

Not one bit.

The only thing that will help is figuring out how to get that money.

Chapter Five

The End-of-the-Year Picnic

In the morning, I crunch a bite of Coral's homemade granola cereal with soy milk.

"May I borrow your bike again today?" she asks me. "Coho needs mine."

The memory of Coral's kale-clad body straddling my bicycle seat makes me nauseated. I stop eating the cereal. I'm not sure I ever want to ride my bike again. "Sure."

"Before you go, MacKenna, Hank and I have a little gift for you, for continuing to seventh grade."

A gift?

Coral holds out a small brown paper bag. I cautiously take the bag and unroll the top. I reach inside and pull out a cell phone. A flip phone. A dinosaur relic, to be precise. It's smaller than my palm.

Coral claps and jumps up and down. "We thought you would love this, MacKenna. And there's more good news!"

Hank and Coral reach into their hip pockets, and together, they pull out matching flip phones, waving them in the air.

"Coho refurbished these little gizmos for us. He also connected us with a carrier." Hank pauses and looks at Coho, who steps into the kitchen. "Is that what you call it?"

Coho nods.

"And we have a family plan for all three of these telephones," Hank explains.

"Yes! One hundred minutes each month and one hundred texts," Coral adds.

"Each?" I ask, clicking the phone open and closed, open and closed.

"No, together as a family unit. It's the one-hundred-one-hundred plan. It's huge."

Huge is an inaccurate word choice, but I don't say it aloud.

I examine the phone's features. Old-school keypad texting and the game Snake. I press the menu key and find my phone number.

Mine.

Coral holds up her opened phone in front of me. "Look! There's a camera too."

I check it out. "I estimate two megapixels, and a limited capacity of photos, which means we'll have to regularly upload them to a computer."

"Keen eye, Mac," Coho says.

"Is that uploading hard to do?" Coral asks me.

I squint at her. "Yes, because we don't have a computer."

"Those flip phones are retro now," Coho says. "Celebs actually crave them."

Retro? Hmmm . . . I wonder how much this phone might be worth. Well under five hundred dollars, but maybe . . . a hundred? I snap the device shut.

"It's more plastic than I'm comfortable with, but Hank and I knew this would be perfect for you, MacKenna."

I've been asking for a phone for two years. This isn't the phone I would choose for myself, but at least I can finally text!

I can't help but wonder whether Hank and Coral are turning a corner. It's a wide, gradually curving corner, and for a nanosecond I consider asking them about coding camp.

Then Hank raises his phone and says, "This is still a screen, Mac, so we don't want you to overuse it and suffer from eyestrain."

Okay, maybe there's no corner.

But I smile at my technology challenged parents. "Thanks."

During a short break between our final math class and final reading class, I slide my flip phone out of my pocket and show Willa and Brie.

Willa laughs and grabs it from my hand, flicking it open and snapping it closed. "This is so cute, Mac. It's a little flipper! Listen to this." She plays with my phone and wiggles her shoulders: *click, click, click, click.*

"Let me see it." Brie takes the phone from Willa. "Oh, I think I've seen these keypads. So, when you want to type a *B*, you hit two twice."

"Right," I say, "then tap three sevens for *R*. Then tap three fours for *I*, and then two threes for *E*. That's your name. It's kind of inefficient."

"But you have a phone! Willa and I can text you this summer."

I take my little flipper from Brie just as Joey Marino breezes past us. My face muscles tense. Joey locks eyes with me, and I think he smiles. He doesn't say anything to me, though, and I shouldn't be surprised by that. But I wonder if he's talked to anyone else and told them what he saw at the statue.

No one has said anything to me.

Yet.

That afternoon, the sixth-grade students walk three blocks to nearby Brooklyn Park for our end-of-the-year picnic. It's one of the school traditions, and all families are invited. I didn't remind Hank and Coral this morning, hoping they wouldn't remember. They're unpredictable at school events. Coral once vocally protested the excessive use of new paper at a fall open house. Afterward, she sponsored a paper recycling drive, encouraging families to bring in usable sheets of paper from home for the school to use. Hank once offered an afterschool drumming class. He signed me up. The only others who joined were Willa and Brie, but after one class, they said they had swimming and ballet classes and couldn't come anymore. I used to love drumming with Hank. He made me a small drum for my tiny hands. We used to sit together on my futon island, banging our skins. Coral would join us and sing, but that was a long time ago, before I was *Bongo Girl*.

I hear quiet music as we near the park. So many parents are there, sitting in lawn chairs around the play structure and picnic tables. I discover the source of the music. Hank sits on the grass tapping his favorite tabor, and Coho is next to him, strumming a guitar. Coral spies me. She stands, waves her arms, and owl-hoots at me.

Behind me, I hear snickers from my classmates. "*Hoo-hoo*. You're being bird called, Hippie Chicken."

I groan and slowly make my way toward the embarrassing trio. At least Coral is wearing clothes.

Hank thumps the drum sandwiched between his knees three times as I sit down, *ba-dum-dum*.

"Why's he here?" I whisper.

"It's a celebration! Coho wanted to contribute." Hank thumps the drum three more times, *ba-dum-dum*.

35

I feel the other families staring at us.

Coral pats my leg. "I love these community celebrations, MacKenna. Hank and I are so pleased to take part." Her skin smells like the lavender-sage incense she burned this morning.

I pull up my knees and hug them to my chest. The sooner this day is over, the better.

Brie sits with her extended family of aunts and uncles at a picnic table. Mr. Vo is cheerfully pouring small paper cups of something thick and orange. I watch Brie drink four cups. Her mother watches too with an intense, disapproving look. She's small but athletic looking and wears makeup and a stunning purple dress.

I shoot a quick glance at Coral. Her eyes are closed. Her head weaves back and forth, her dreadlocks and plastic bits swaying with her.

I once asked Coral why she never put me in swimming like Brie. She said, "Athletics are too competitive and confining, MacKenna. They do not allow for youthful enlightenment."

But Brie seems youthful enough to me.

Willa sits unusually still on a low beach chair between her amazing, all-American parents. She seems worried or distracted, and I wonder why. She's got parents with *real* jobs, a big house, and two cars. Parents who wear clothes . . .

on all occasions. Mrs. Moore gazes toward the kids on the play structure. Willa's little sister, Becca, is swinging on the monkey bars, but Mrs. Moore doesn't seem to be paying attention. Mr. Moore is glued to his phone, both thumbs swiftly tapping the screen.

I look at Hank, who's softly tapping his drum. There's chicken feed in his beard.

I sneak a glance at Coho. He's slumped over the guitar, apparently napping.

At last, Mr. Bellini, our principal, raises his hands to his mouth. "Families, will you gather around, please."

Parents rise from their chairs, and students move toward the red oak tree where Mr. Bellini stands.

"As you know, Winterhill issues an award to one student each year who takes the most initiative toward improving our school community. I'd like to honor that student now, at our family picnic."

Coral sighs and places her hands on her heart.

"The recipient of this award will have his or her name engraved on our school plaque in the front hallway," Mr. Bellini continues.

The students begin a drumroll on their legs.

So does Hank. On his drum. *Ba-dum-ba-dum-ba-dum-ba-dum.*

I scan my classmates, wondering who will receive the

award. Maybe Pilar. She's always taking out the recycling bins from classrooms. Maybe Aditi, who's always making posters about upcoming events.

"The student honored today has been the quiet brain-child behind several improvements to Winterhill this year, improvements that have benefitted our entire school community." Mr. Bellini pauses and scans the crowd before him. "This student brought us the water-filtration systems in the hallway, the food composting program in the kitchen, and the free food table in our cafeteria."

Coral grabs my hand and squeezes it. "How colossal."

Coral wants me to win this award, but these are not my projects.

"This year's Winterhill Community Award goes to . . . Joey Marino!"

Willa turns and looks at me, her eyebrows lifted. She was right yesterday when she said Joey was like a phantom. We don't know where he is or what he's thinking, and we obviously *never* know what he's planning or doing.

The audience is silent. Everyone looks around for Joey Marino, but he isn't here.

Coral throws her arms in the air and claps over her head, prompting the rest of the crowd to clap too. And then she whoops like a crane.

I cringe. "Please don't."

My classmates glance her way, snickers on their faces.

And then, almost magically, Joey Marino materializes from the middle of the crowd. He drifts toward Mr. Bellini, cloud-like, in his uniform of black jeans, gray shirt, and combat boots, his expression unreadable.

"Oh, MacKenna," Coral gushes. "This is such an honor for him."

Hank nods in agreement.

Coho plucks some notes on his guitar strings.

I keep my eye on Joey, expecting he might disappear as suddenly as he appeared. He shakes Mr. Bellini's hand and takes a certificate. Mr. Bellini leans over and whispers something to Joey, but Joey shakes his head, and Mr. Bellini nods in return.

"Well, our honoree does not have words of wisdom to share with you." Mr. Bellini smiles. "So, I'll just thank him again for his contributions that will be experienced by all Winterhill students present and future. Thank you, Joey." He firmly shakes Joey's hand once more.

Coral wipes a tear from her cheek. If only she were as moved by my school projects, the robotic arm I created, the Pac-Man-like game.

She whoops again, which catches Joey's attention. He turns and sees her . . . and me. He looks long and hard. Does he recognize her?

I attempt to inch away, dropping my head, but Coral reaches for me and tugs my arm. "MacKenna, do you know him? Is he a friend of yours?" She points at Joey.

All I can do is shake my head.

He's not a friend.

And I'm pretty sure *no one* knows him.

Chapter Six

The Hawthorne Street Food Carts

Mr. Bellini wishes us well in the summer months, reminding us to read lots. He tells us to be sure to clean up our trash and then we can head back to school to collect our belongings.

Coral wraps her arm around my shoulder. "MacKenna, that was fantastic. Hank and I will converse with the other parents and introduce them to Coho, and then we'll celebrate with you and your friends. Maybe Joey can come over for dinner."

"No!" I don't want them celebrating with my friends and having dinner with Joey Marino. These do not sound like good ideas.

"Why not? Do you have plans?" Hank asks.

"Um . . . well, Brie and Willa and I thought we'd stay late and help clean up all the hallways." It's the only thing I can think of to get them to leave.

Coral slaps her hand on her heart. "Joey's community

spirit has already got to you." She pulls me in for a hug.

"Of course." I fake a smile and squirm out of her arms. "I'll see you at home."

I hurry ahead to catch the group of students returning to Winterhill. Once we arrive, I go to my math classroom, where I collect my binder and desk items and shove them into my shoulder bag. I wave goodbye to my teacher before leaving the room.

The hallway's crowded with students and parents, but all I want is to forget this day, find Willa and Brie, and leave. Then I can go back to figuring out how to raise five hundred dollars.

A few classmates slap my back as they pass.

"Have fun with your chickens this summer!"

"They are *not* my chickens," I yell back. I'm not in an ignoring frame of mind. I'm in a money-making mind-set now.

"Maybe I'll swing by that big festival of yours, Earth Child."

"Enjoy yourself," I say. "I won't be there."

One boy thumps his thighs, *ba-dum-dum*, and laughs out loud. "Bongo Girl, tell your dad, Nice drum!"

I do manage to ignore that jab and keep moving down the hallway. Then I see him.

Joey Marino.

He's standing alone in the hallway near a table, staring

into his backpack. No one is near him to offer hugs or good-byes. His long wavy hair looks dull and flat.

The sight of him completely alone makes me swallow. Hard.

Phantom Boy.

Have I ever seen him with a friend?

With a parent?

As soon as I think that, a woman rushes toward Joey. Her dark hair has streaks of gray, and it's pulled into a tight bun. She wears a drab brown polyester dress and white tennis shoes. I can see a plastic name tag pinned under her collar. It says *Patsy's Diner* in a large font, but I can't read her name below. Is *she* Joey's mom?

The woman speaks to him, but his back is to me, so I can't see his expression. She hugs Joey quickly, smooths the hair from his face, and then rushes off again down the hall-way. Joey doesn't watch her go.

I pause to spy a bit longer.

He begins stuffing items from the table into his back-pack. First some folders, then a couple of books, and lastly his phone. I don't know why I'm watching him. Is it because he saw Coral at the picnic? He looked at her as she whooped and hollered for him. Did he recognize her . . . with clothes on?

Just as I'm thinking all this, Joey turns toward me and sees me staring. He stares back with his semitranslucent face. Neither of us says a word or moves an inch.

Then he raises his hand and waves, just like he did yesterday at the statue near the naked bikers.

I should wave back, but I turn away from him instead and set out to find Willa and Brie. As I shove open the front door of the school, I see them, waiting for me by the flagpole.

"Mac!" Willa leaps in front of me and grabs my elbow, pulling me north on 14th Avenue. "Brie, I didn't get any of your dad's drink. What was it?"

"Mango lassi. Mom says it's bad for me. She says swimmers shouldn't consume too much dairy and sugar. It causes bloating."

"It looked delicious," I say.

"It is," Brie agrees.

"Hey, was that your cousin James with your parents?" Willa asks. "He looked different."

"He is different. He goes by Coho now. He's like a clone of Hank."

"Wait!" Willa jumps in front of me. "He was with your mom yesterday at the statue! He was riding naked too."

"Can we just forget what we saw?" I ask. "I can't even think about riding my bike again this summer."

"You could use my bike," Brie suggests. "All I'm doing this summer is swimming. I have no use for it."

"At least you enjoy swimming," I say. "There's nothing

about summer I enjoy."

But Brie doesn't answer. Her eyes are fixed on the sidewalk.

We stop at the busy Powell Boulevard intersection, waiting for the crossing light. "What about your coding camp?" Willa asks.

I let out a heavy sigh. "My plan was to talk to James. I figured he could convince Hank and Coral it was a good thing. But now he's all *technology and money are evil*, so there goes that idea. Anyway, I still don't know how I would pay for the camp, even if Hank and Coral agreed to let me go."

"Sell your bike!" Willa offers.

My eyes pop. How did I not think of that? It's the most expensive item I own, even though it was secondhand when I got it. But I know it's not worth five hundred dollars. Maybe a hundred, tops.

"That's a great idea," I say, "but what other ideas do you have?"

"Get a job," Willa offers. She begins skipping and swinging her arms as we cross the street.

"No one hires twelve-year-olds," Brie says.

"You could babysit," Willa suggests. "Maybe for my sister."

"Really?" I ask. "But don't you do that?"

"Yeah, well, I can't all summer, I mean I have to . . ."

"You have to what?"

Willa stops skipping. "Forget it," she says quickly. "Hey, how about this for an idea?" Willa grins and pulls a stack of bills from her pocket. "Dad gave me spending money. Who wants to hit the food carts? My treat!"

"I'm in." Nothing can take me away from my worries like food outside of Coral's kitchen.

Portland's like the food cart capital of the universe. There're hundreds of carts all over the city, eight-by-sixteen-foot trailers, plopped down in parking lots. Instant street-side, order-and-go restaurants. Whatever you feel like eating, there's a food cart for your cravings.

As we walk through the archway of the Hawthorne cart pod, I inhale deeply, filling my nostrils with the food scents of these carts, clustered together, like an outdoor mall food court.

I immediately head to Manny's Grill for a half-pound bacon cheeseburger on a *white* bun. It's a carnivore's dream, provided there are plenty of napkins.

"I'm getting a baked potato," Brie says.

"Look." Willa points. "A newbie."

I follow Willa's finger and notice the addition to the Hawthorne carts: a white trailer with the flag of Italy on the side. I can't see a name, but there's a chalkboard easel nearby that reads *Handmade Mini-Pizzas*.

"Hey, kids, try my pizzas!" A white-haired man yells at us from the window of the trailer. "I make them fresh, right

in front of you. *Delizioso!* Check out my topping selection."
He talks fast with his flour-covered hands and motions to
another chalkboard hanging inside. It's an impressive setup.
A real stone oven inside a trailer.

"Okay," Willa says. "I'll take one with pepperoni and
olives. And also a lemonade."

"I'll have cheese and mushrooms," Brie says. "And just
water to drink."

"And you?" The man points at me.

I had my mind set on a bacon burger, but the smell coming from this guy's oven is amazing. It's worth a try.

"I'll take the meat combo." And then, remembering
that Willa has money to cover the tab, I add, "And a Coke,
please."

The man freezes for just a moment, but then gives me
a wink.

"If you like my pizzas, you tell your friends and family,
okay? My name's Lorenzo." He tosses a ball of dough in the
air and catches it, forming a cloud of flour in front of his
face. He slathers garlicky olive oil all over the pizzas and
generously piles on the cheese.

Willa, Brie, and I step back and slurp on our drinks while
we wait. I see a stray dime on the ground, and I scoop it up
and pocket it. Every coin counts when it comes to bringing
in money. Brie moans about her summer swim schedule and
her upcoming meet. Willa's phone buzzes with incoming

texts, and she responds to each one. I wonder who she's texting, but before I can ask, we hear a timer ding, and we move back toward Lorenzo's window. He lines three paper plates with checkered tissue paper and slides the mini-pizzas on top.

"Enjoy, new friends!" he says and quickly helps the next customers in line.

We carry our pizzas to the rows of picnic tables in the center of the cart pod and start chowing down. I practically inhale my first bite of sausage and cheese.

"Hey, look." Brie points at my paper plate. "Lorenzo left you a note."

I lift the red-checkered tissue paper. There *is* a note, scribbled in black ink.

Got a chip on your shoulder? Put a hat on instead.
It may feel a bit grey, but upstairs you'll be fed.

Chapter Seven

The Missing Mysterious Note

"What is this?"

I shove the tissue paper toward Willa. She reads it, mumbling the words, "'but upstairs you'll be fed.'" She shrugs and hands it to Brie.

"Do you think Lorenzo wrote this?" Brie asks.

"Probably. He was the only one in his cart." I take the tissue paper from Brie and read it again.

"I think it's a riddle." I love riddles. They remind me of writing computer programs. You break them down into parts to make sense of the whole. When you get an ERROR message, you just try again. It's beautiful, logical problem-solving.

Willa tears a piece of crust off her pizza, chews it, then speaks. "Maybe. But maybe it's nothing."

I continue to stare at the note, reading it and rereading. I'm startled by the loud clang of a metal travel mug hitting the picnic table next to me. I turn to my left to see a gray shirt and a pale face.

Joey Marino.

Just four or five feet away from me.

I cough a bit on the pizza crumbs lingering in my throat. Where in the world did he come from?

Joey gives me a flicker of a glance, but then he eyes the tissue paper with the mysterious note.

I look up at Willa and Brie sitting across from me and jerk my head to the left to get them to turn, to see Joey.

But when my friends look, Joey's no longer there. He's moved to a different picnic table, one farther away from us.

He lifts his combat boots over the bench and sits across from an old woman at the end of the table. I think she's homeless. I've seen her wandering around these carts before, messy gray bun, stocking cap, and layers and layers of clothes.

"It's Joey Marino, you guys," I whisper.

"It is?" Willa squints toward him. "Hey, did you guys know he had done all that stuff at school?"

"I knew about the water fountains, but not the other projects," Brie says.

Joey hands the woman his travel mug. She reaches for it and cradles it in her palms. Her hands quiver as she lifts the mug to her mouth.

"Do you think he knows her?" I ask.

"Maybe he's working on a new community project," Willa says. "Something to help homeless people."

Joey pulls his phone out of his pocket. He taps the screen and shows the woman. She points and gestures. I wonder what he's showing her.

Willa and Brie return to eating their pizza, and I pretend not to be interested in Joey Marino and his conversation, but I keep sneaking glances.

The woman pushes the mug back to Joey and touches his hand. Then she rises from the bench. He waves at her.

"Are you both done?" Willa asks. "Let's take a long route home."

I shove the last bit of pizza crust into my mouth and stand up. We take our plates and napkins to the trash cans and dump them.

"Before we go, I want to ask Lorenzo about that note," I say. "I want to know what it means."

"Where is the note?" Brie asks.

My hands are empty. Did I throw it away? I whip back toward the garbage can when I spy Joey Marino again, back at the table we were sitting at. He's folding the red-checkered tissue paper with the strange riddle. He tucks it into his pocket and walks away.

"Did you guys see that? Joey has my note." I wave my

finger as Joey leaves the Hawthorne cart pod.

Brie links my elbow. "Forget about it, Mac. I'm sure it meant nothing."

But I'm not so sure, and I want it back. I want to program Joey Marino to spin around, to give back that note. *Turn left 180 degrees. Forward 500 steps.*

But Joey has already vanished.

Willa links my other elbow. "Sorry, Mac. Mystery here one moment. Mystery gone the next."

"Come on." Brie pulls on my arm. "It's only four thirty, and it's the first afternoon of summer."

I don't budge. The message on the checkered paper loops in my brain: *Got a chip on your shoulder? Put a hat on instead. It may feel a bit grey, but upstairs you'll be fed.* It doesn't matter that Joey Marino has the note because I won't forget what's on it. I know those words mean something. I have to find out what it is.

"I'm going back."

"Oh, come on," Willa whines. "Let it go. Time for some summer dancing." She throws her arms out wide and shimmies.

But I ignore Willa and return to the pizza cart.

"Hey! Lorenzo?"

"Oh! My best new customer. You liked my pizza so much you returned." He kisses his flour-coated fingers, then throws the kiss in the air. *"Eccellente!"*

"Your pizzas were great, but I didn't come back for more. I wanted to ask about the note you gave me—"

"And which pizza do you want this time? How about Classico? Fresh mozzarella with basil and tomato." His flour-dusted lips smile at me.

"No, I don't want another pizza. Sorry, but—"

"Oh, I'm sorry too." He turns away and grabs some dough.

"Can I ask you about that note?" I try again.

"I don't know what you mean." Lorenzo keeps his head down. "Do you want another pizza?"

This stinks. I'm going to have to buy his information.

I shove my hands into my jeans pockets and feel my new, yet ancient, flipper phone, some lint, and the single dime I picked up off the ground earlier.

"Hey, Lorenzo." It's Willa's voice. She and Brie are back. "We'll take one of those Classicos."

Willa holds up a five-dollar bill for the pizza.

Thank you, I mouth.

"One Classico coming up," Lorenzo announces.

I tap my fingers on Lorenzo's window counter for a few moments, pondering how to broach the subject of the mysterious message again. "So, about that note? You wrote it, right?"

"Yes."

"What does it mean, exactly? Why'd you give it to me?"

Brie and Willa lean in closer now to the cart window.

Lorenzo spirals the dough in the air and catches it on his fist, lowering it to the work surface. "You ordered the right pizza, so you got the note."

I turn to Brie and lift an eyebrow.

She shrugs.

"Is it a riddle?" I ask.

"Of course it's a riddle." He tosses some leafy stuff on the dough. "And it's a clue to the hunt."

"What hunt?"

"The Portland Food Cart Association Treasure Hunt. You visit the right carts around the city. You order the right foods, then you get clues. Collect all the clues, and you win the prize. *Semplice.*"

"What's the prize?" Willa asks.

Lorenzo places tomatoes on the leafy stuff. "Two thousand dollars."

Wait.

Two. Thousand. Dollars?

For collecting all the clues?

"Are you making this up?" I blurt.

"No. It's a real hunt and a real prize." Lorenzo moves to his window and begins whispering to us, even though no one else is near. "Food Cart Association put out ten clues at ten carts. First person to turn in all the clues at the right time and the right cart wins the prize."

"Why are you whispering?" Brie asks.

"It's a secret hunt. The association wants to see how well it gets around without any social media or advertisements." Lorenzo winks.

"When did it start?" I ask.

"June twelfth."

That's five days ago. I wonder how many people already know? "When does it end?"

"June twenty-sixth." Lorenzo scoops up the pizza with a huge wooden spatula and slides it into his stone oven.

"If I find all the clues, when and where do I turn them in?"

"Can't tell you that. Check out the website." Lorenzo waves us away with his fingers before grabbing another ball of dough. "Your Classico is ready in five minutes. Oh, and tell your friends about my new cart!"

Chapter Eight

Plea Bargaining

I'm practically levitating as we wait for the pizza.

Ten clues.

Collect them all.

Win two thousand dollars!

That much money will buy me the coding camp, and I'd have enough left to buy a laptop and an actual smart phone!

Eight weeks of coding camp means less time with the chickens and Coral's vegetables. I could avoid almost the entire ridiculous Mother Earth Festival. This is all so perfectly perfect.

I jump in front of my friends. "You guys! Let's do the hunt."

"Seriously, Mac." Brie laughs a little. "There are probably hundreds of people already looking for those clues."

"But maybe not. He said it was secret. Don't you see?

Winning this money would get me to coding camp. It's my exit from Hank and Coral's world to the real world."

I hold my mouth open, waiting for a response.

"Yeah, I don't know," Willa says. "I'm not so sure about this." She steps to Lorenzo's to grab our steaming-hot pizza.

"Think about it." I motion for Willa and Brie to follow me back to a picnic table. We all sit down. "If we do it together, we can split the prize." I calculate quickly in my head. "That's six hundred sixty-six dollars for each of us. And sixty-six cents!" Still plenty of money for the coding camp.

Willa shakes her head. She pulls out her phone and reads a text.

"Willa, what else could you possibly have to do in the next few days?" I ask.

She tucks her phone back into her front pocket. "I have a few things going on."

I let out a heavy sigh.

"Mac," Brie says, "my parents wouldn't be happy with me wandering all over the city, looking for clues at food carts. They'd say it's a waste of time."

"But your dad's a chef. He loves all the food carts. Besides, they don't need to know what you're *really* doing. We'll come up with a good story. We'll say we're doing some research, like a summer study. Parents eat that stuff up." I smile at Brie and punch her lightly on the forearm.

She laughs. "It kind of does sound fun. And I like food, and it involves eating."

"And our free city bus passes last through June, so we don't have to pay for transportation," I add. "Come on, you guys. The hunt ends on June twenty-sixth. That's only nine days. It isn't like it goes *all* summer."

Brie turns to Willa. "What do you say?"

Willa's zoned out, her eyes glassy. It's the same look she wore earlier at the park, sitting between her parents. She's tearing a napkin into tiny little pieces.

"Willa? What's up with you?" I ask.

"What?" She finally looks at me.

"Are you in?" I say.

"In what?" She turns her face toward me and then Brie.

"In the hunt with us," Brie says.

I sneak a glance at Brie that says *Is she okay?*

"Come on." I try to encourage Willa. "It's a two-thousand-dollar prize! We need you."

Willa opens her mouth like she's going to say something, but nothing comes out. And then, a switch in her brain seems to flick on. Her eyes open wide, and she gets off the bench and does a little shuffling box step. "Okay," she says. "But if I'm in, I'm in to win."

Now that's more like it. I grin at my friend, watching

her box step some more.

I reach my hand out, palm down. Brie puts hers on top. Willa follows. "In to win!" we yell at the same time, throwing our arms up.

Chapter Nine

Summer Plans for All

One thing I know for sure is that the internet will be my friend for this food cart hunt, but my little flipper phone doesn't offer that. Neither does my technology-free household. The public libraries are my only option, and lucky for me, the Belmont Library is close by and stays open until eight p.m. most nights. I walk there after Brie, Willa, and I leave the Hawthorne carts. I tap out a short text to Hank and Coral letting them know where I am. I'm not completely convinced that they know how to read texts yet, but at least I can say I contacted them. Then I write down the clue on a bookmark while it's still in my head.

Got a chip on your shoulder? Put a hat on instead.
It may feel a bit grey, but upstairs you'll be fed.

I spot an open computer and log on. I need to find that website that Lorenzo mentioned. Right away I find one called Portland Food Cart Association, and another called Portland Food Carts and Friends. I comb around for info on the hunt, but just like Lorenzo said, there's no advertisements or announcements. I guess it's good that it's a secret hunt. The fewer people who know, the better chance I have! I scroll through the newsfeed on the association's website, but it seems to just be a listing of new carts and times. I do discover a list of food types and the carts that serve those styles all around the city. That will be helpful. I highlight the information and show my student ID card to the librarian, so I can print the cart lists for free.

Tonight, I'll study the clue and the list of carts. I know I can figure this out. I'll just go word by word, step by step, like writing a code. Simple!

In the morning, I stare at the poster Mrs. Naberhaus gave me, *Girls Are Supercoders*, that I hung on the wall above my head. I reach up and put my whole palm on the poster, whispering the words. Today, on the first day of summer, with the food cart hunt ahead of me, I believe these words. I have to be a supercoder to find all these clues.

Emptying an old folder from school, I place the list of carts, the clue, and some blank paper inside, then tuck the folder in my shoulder bag before heading outside to confront the three leghorns and the illegal Poppy.

Back in the kitchen with the four eggs, my brain spins with the clue.

Chip, hat, grey, upstairs. I know those words are key.

What type of food is it referring to?

And even if I know the type of food, what specifically do I order?

"Happy summer, Mac!" Hank enters the kitchen and slaps my back. "Gather the eggs already?"

"Done."

Hank lifts one of the brown eggs out of the basket and sniffs it. "I never get tired of fresh eggs."

"I've noticed."

"Add kale, please!" Coral yells from the living room, probably just beginning her morning yoga.

"Mac, are you ready to hear my plans for our summer?"

"Is it about your festival?"

"It's preparation for the festival." Hank cracks an egg and separates the shell, letting the insides ooze into a bowl. "Today, you and I and Coho are going to start building a fence around Coral's garden. Mr. Z said we could take down his old fence and use that lumber. That's our first step." Hank grins at me.

"Why does Coral need a fence?"

"Oh, Coral doesn't need a fence—her vegetables do."

Hank whips his eggs with a fork.

"What?" I feel wary about this project already.

"Her vegetables will need protection."

"Protection? How many people have you and Coral invited to your festival?"

Hank laughs. "I'm not talking about protection from people, I'm talking about protection from the—"

"Hank, wait!" Coral hurries into the kitchen and grabs Hank's elbow. She whispers into his ear.

Hank pulls back. "You think?"

Coral leans in and whispers something else.

"I see your point," Hank finally says. "I'll wait."

"You'll wait for what?" I ask.

"For the summer plan reveal. It's going to be epic!" Hank drums the countertops, *ba-dum-dum*. "Believe me."

I do not believe him, but I push my shoulders back and state, "I have a plan to reveal this summer too."

Coral pulls up a chair and peers at me. "Ooh, tell us."

"I'm going to be doing some research on the food carts of Portland." It's the same line I told Brie to use on her parents.

"Food carts?" Hank and Coral say at the same time.

Coho wanders into the kitchen, grabs some tea, and sits down with us.

I need to make this plan sound legit. I must appeal to their do-gooder, socially conscious ways. I begin my lie. "I'm doing a study to determine which food carts are using only fresh, local ingredients on their menus."

Coho shoots me a doubtful look. His brow is wrinkled. Does he know I'm lying?

Then Coral sighs and takes both my hands in hers. "MacKenna, this is colossal." She beams at me. "All of those projects Joey Marino has done must have moved you."

Wait. What is she talking about? Joey Marino's projects?

I gulp. "Um, sure."

Coral can believe whatever she wants. She doesn't need to know that the two-thousand-dollar prize is the only thing moving me.

Coral pats my cheek. "I adore this spirit in you! We can put your results on our community board, advocating for those sustainable food carts."

I nod, yet I feel a gap inside me widen when Coral smiles. I don't know if it's because my story is a lie, or because what I want my world to be is so far away from what she wants.

"Maybe you could ask about travel distance too, Mac," Hank suggests. "From farm to mouth in the fewest steps. That's the key to fresh food."

"Right. Decrease the massive carbon footprint." I swallow some sarcasm.

"I like your mind-set." Hank squeezes me around the shoulders. "All right. I'll give you a one-day pass on the fence building, but that's it. Coho and I'll need your help tomorrow."

Coho winks at me, which makes me swallow again, but this time with a little guilt. For today, though, I'm free.

"Is your friend Joey helping you?" Coral asks.

"What? No. Joey isn't exactly a friend of mine. Willa and Brie are helping, though."

Coral gets up from the table. "Here are some zucchini muffins for you all to take while you research today, and I'll make some kale chips this afternoon too."

After the incident at the Joan of Arc statue and discovering where Coral puts her kale, I want nothing to do with it entering my digestive system. I'm about to tell Coral no thanks, when my head has a magnificent spark. I've found the elusive computer command, the missing step that solves the problem.

Chips!

Chips are what I'm supposed to order to get the next clue!

It's brilliant.

"Thanks, Coral!" I stand up and kiss her cheek, which makes her smile, and I dash back to my futon island, grabbing my folder with my notes and the clue.

Got a chip on your shoulder? Put a hat on instead.
It may feel a bit grey, but upstairs you'll be fed.

I have a hunch about something. I find an old dictionary on the bookshelf in the living room and look up the word *grey*. In America we use the spelling *g-r-a-y*, but according to this dictionary *g-r-e-y* is the common spelling in the United Kingdom. England!

And England is where everyone wears fancy *hats*.

And in England, *chips* are what we call French fries, but they're potatoes, not kale.

This clue is telling me that I'm supposed to order chips at an English food cart.

I skim the list I printed yesterday from the library, looking specifically for English-style food. It can only be the double-decker bus cart at the Rose City pod on Sandy Boulevard. The double-decker bus would explain the *upstairs*.

I locate my little flipper and tediously tap out a group text to Willa and Brie. 7777666555 . . . thirty-three clicks on the keypad, and then I hit Send: Solved the clue.

I knew I could do this!

Girls ARE Supercoders.

Chapter Ten

The Double-decker Bus

Willa, Brie, and I take the 75 bus to Sandy Boulevard and walk the remaining way to the Rose City carts, which sit in a parking lot next to a popular bike store. I quickly count ten carts framing a small, uncovered eating area in the middle of the lot. The largest trailer serves Russian food and has a big poster board showing pictures of their various dishes. There's also a gluten-free food place, a Vietnamese cart, and one serving crab chowder.

A lot of people mill around, reading the menus. I wonder if any of them are our competition.

The red double-decker bus is tucked between a Chinese place and a cart that's called Good Eats. In the front window of the bus is a poster with the Union Jack flag, and printed below that it reads: *Today's Special: Seafood Platter $12.00.*

"Twelve dollars!" I say.

Brie walks up close to the sign and reads the fine print.

"It comes with cod and herring, chips and . . . mushy peas?"

We all curl our lips.

"Here's the main menu." Willa points to a sign next to the order window. We scan the list. There's a one-piece, two-piece, and three-piece fish and chips. One of those *must* hold the next clue. The other items are things like tarts and pasties with no mention of chips.

"What do we get?" Willa asks.

"Here's what I'm thinking. The clue will probably come with a more expensive item. I mean, these carts want to make money, right?"

Willa and Brie nod.

"So, let's cover our bases and order one special, one three-piece fish and chips, and one two-piece."

Willa squints at the menu again.

"I've already done the math. It's thirty dollars, ten for each of us." I tell her.

"Here," Brie says. "Dad always gives me snack money for my swim workouts. I don't always use it." She pulls out two fives from the tiny purse hanging over her shoulder.

I reach into the bottom of my bag and pull out a five and two ones. "These are my only bills, but I have eight bucks in coins. Willa, I'll pay fifteen dollars since I owe you from yesterday."

Silently, I recalculate my life savings: $14.43.

Willa reaches into her shorts pocket and unfolds a five.

I whisper the order to the bus guy because a couple has moved in behind us. We have to keep our eyes open for our competitors. The bus guy hollers the order to someone we can't see.

So much for being secretive.

"Wait." I think through the clue one more time, then glance at the drink menu before turning to Willa. "Do you have two more dollars?"

She pulls out another wad of bills from her pocket and hands me two ones.

You're the best, I mouth to her, and then I lean back in to the bus guy. "We'll also have a large tea. Earl Grey, please."

"There's seating upstairs," the man says as I hand him the money, carefully watching his face for a wink or a smile or some indication that another clue is coming, but he simply adds, "We'll bring the food when it's ready."

We step up the spiral staircase to the top deck of the bus and sit down at one of the four tables. We're the only ones here. This seems hopeful.

About ten minutes later, the man comes up the stairs with our tray of food. "Enjoy, girls!"

Brie takes the special. I grab the three-piece and Willa the two-piece. "Pull out the tissue paper from under the food. That's where the clue will be," I say.

We all do, but our papers have nothing but grease stains.

The napkins are blank too. We check each one.

I slam my fist on the table. "What did we do wrong?"

"Sorry, Mac," Brie says.

"You think it was the one-piece?" Willa asks, carefully inspecting a chip before placing it in her mouth.

I don't answer. I pick up the paper cup of Earl Grey and take a sip. The sleeve around the cup shifts in my palm.

Wait.

Maybe . . .

I take off the sleeve and open it.

And there it is. Handwritten. Two lines.

I hold it up for Willa and Brie to read.

Put a tag in early, then pull up a pad.
While the meat is prepared, a "whiskey's" not bad.

"Mac, you did it!" Willa shouts. "This calls for some dancing. Move out of the way, Brie."

Brie giggles and scoots her chair back, so Willa can glide to the aisle of the bus. She starts her best disco moves, swaying her hips and pointing her fingers up and down. Brie joins her with a few swimming-stroke moves.

Clutching the clue in my hand, I stand up and dramatically holler, "God save the Queen!"

We high-five and dance and clap in the aisle of the double-decker bus, not caring how loud we are or that our food is getting cold. We have another clue!

I'm shuffling toward the stairs of the bus, waving my arms up at the ceiling, when someone appears at the top of the stairs.

I let out a soft scream.

Joey Marino takes a step back. His gray eyes bulge. A stained white apron hangs around his neck.

Why is he suddenly always around?

"Excuse me." He brushes past me, leans over one of the tables, and begins wiping it down with a wet rag. All I can do is continue to stare at him.

"Joey?" Brie finally speaks. "Do you work here?"

He keeps wiping the table and then the chairs. "Just today."

Is this another community service project of his?

Then I notice a piece of cardboard sticking out of the pocket of his apron. It's a cup sleeve, just like the one I'm holding.

My jaw drops open as he wads his rag in his palm and turns to walk down the stairs.

Brie shrugs her shoulders.

Willa says, "*That* was weird. That boy is weird."

I shake my head. "No, he's not weird. I know weird, and he's not that. He's just . . ."

"Phantom boy?" Brie says.

"That's for sure," Willa agrees. "I didn't hear him coming up those steps. Did you?"

"We were kind of loud, and dancing around," I remind them. "But, you guys . . ." I motion for them to sit back down. "I think Joey is doing the hunt. He grabbed the clue from Lorenzo's yesterday when I left it on the table, and today I saw a cup sleeve in his apron pocket."

"So, you think he's our competition?" Willa asks.

"Why don't we just go ask him?" Brie suggests.

I take a bite of a chip. It's still slightly warm. "No. I don't want to ask. I think we just need to keep going. There's three of us, and only one of him. We have a better chance. We already have two clues."

"But so does he," Willa adds.

"Let's just keep working at it," I say.

The truth is, the magically appearing and disappearing Joey Marino makes me worried and nervous, and I don't understand why. He makes me feel like I'm doing something wrong.

But I have to sweep all that worry away because I want to win this food cart hunt.

I want to go to this computer camp. I'm tired of being Hippie Chick and Bongo Girl. I want a new identity, like Supercoder.

Winning this money is my only hope.

Chapter Eleven

The Division Street Cart Pod

When I get home, I see a pile of beat-up lumber in the backyard. Hank, Coral, and Coho are sitting on the grass. Hank is softly drumming while Coho strums his guitar. Coral is sitting lotus style, eyes closed. Livie, Divie, or maybe Bolivie pecks around the dirt in the garden.

I retreat to my futon island, so I can study the second clue and plot my strategy. I wonder if Joey Marino has more than two clues. No. I can't worry about that now. I must stay focused.

I pull a sheet of scratch paper from my hunt folder to sketch out my timeline. I have two clues. Tomorrow's Saturday, June 19, which means we have exactly eight more days to find the remaining eight clues before the June 26 deadline. That's one clue each day. The first clue took me only a day to solve. I simply have to keep up that pace.

I decide to change my tactic on this clue and try a new algorithm. I'll visit nearby cart pods and check out their menus, looking for connections to the key words. I tap out a text to Willa and Brie: Meet me at the Division carts tomorrow at 11.

This seems like a good place to start.

Brie responds right away: Tomorrow's out. At a swim meet. Wish me luck!

I should have known that. She always has weekend meets. I respond with *Good luck*, knowing it isn't needed. Brie can outswim a school of tuna.

Willa finally answers an hour later: Can't. Doing stuff with my dad.

That's odd. Willa doesn't hang out with her dad much. I text back: What stuff?

Willa: Movie.

Me: When does it end?

Willa: Don't know.

Me: Have any time for the hunt tomorrow?

Willa: I'm out tomorrow. Sorry, Mac.

I pause a moment and reread Willa's texts. Something doesn't seem right with her. She's been acting strange for a while now.

I snap my flipper shut and tuck it into my jeans pocket. I study the cup sleeve with clue number two and jot down the key words: *tag, early, pad, meat, whiskey*. I have to think of the links to these words. I have to *de-code*. It's only a puzzle to solve.

I can do this.

In the morning, I'm tediously picking the collard greens out of Coral's scrambled eggs with a fork, when Hank and Coho come into the kitchen from the backyard. "Mac, there's a bucket of fasteners by the garden that we pulled out of Mr. Z's fencing lumber. We need you to sort through it and set aside the screws and nails that aren't stripped or bent."

I slump in my chair. "Wouldn't it be easier to just go buy new screws?"

"Now why would we do that?" Hank scoops eggs out of the skillet for himself and then Coho. "Reduce. Reuse. Recycle."

I can't count the number of times Hank and Coral have said this.

Reduce. Reuse. Recycle.

They used to sing me a little song about it.

"You know that our national economy depends on people buying new products, right?" I learned about this in social studies. "If we buy things, they have to make more of those things. That provides jobs. Jobs give people money, so they can continue to buy things. That's how the economic circle works."

Hank stares at me.

Coho chuckles. "You have a smart kid, Hank. She's forging her path."

He's right about that. I'm forging a path to computer coding camp. It's another circle, really. Teach girls to code. We create great things. People buy what we create. We continue to create. It's an infinite loop of progress.

But Hank doesn't see the real path that's in front of me. He still sees the one he and Coral created for me when I was born. The one they think I'll walk down. Hank and Coral will never change. They live in their own infinite loop of weirdness. And now Coho lives it with them.

I find the bucket of hardware outside and put on a pair of Coral's gardening gloves. One at a time I pick out the rusty, bent, and stripped screws and nails and toss them into a cardboard box. It's a laborious hour of sorting, but I finish.

Back inside the living room, I grab my shoulder bag, put my hunt folder and some coins from my dwindling savings inside, and slip away, walking toward Division Street. I chant the clue in my head over and over again:

Put a tag in early, then pull up a pad.
While the meat is prepared, a "whiskey's" not bad.

Put a tag in early. What does that mean? It seems key.

The Division Street cart pod is buzzing with the early lunch crowd. The carts are bunched side by side in a mazelike formation. I enter through a small flower-lined walkway and glance around. The only thing I know for sure is that I'm looking for a cart that has meat on its menu. The first trailer is Mediterranean Vegetarian, which rules it out immediately. There's a sausage and fondue place that doesn't seem right. Two Thai carts are possibilities, but I keep zigzagging through the trailers.

I stop near Greg's Grilled Cheese and sniff. It smells delicious. Two guys look over the menu, their heads together, their eyes on their phones. I move closer so I'm standing right behind the pair. I pretend to look over their shoulders at the grilled cheese menu while I eavesdrop.

The shaggy-haired guy says, "I don't think it's Swiss. Jack is the key."

The other guy has a dark scar on his cheek. He's shaking his head. "But which?"

I lean in a bit to hear them better.

Scarface guy points to the menu board. "Number Four is Monterey Jack and Number Five is pepper jack."

My eyelids pop open wide. These two are in the hunt! My spine straightens, and I glance around. Greg's Grilled Cheese must have one of the clues I need.

I may have gasped a little because Shaggy and Scarface

turn around and say, "Hey, why don't you go ahead of us. We haven't decided yet."

"Oh, I'm just looking, trying to figure out which cart to try," I lie.

"Know what you mean," Shaggy answers. "That German place has killer brats."

"Thanks." I know full well that I won't be ordering a brat or anything else. I won't spend my loose change on any food unless I know it will lead me to another clue.

Shaggy and Scarface step off to the side of the cart and continue their discussion.

I know I can't move any closer to them. They'd be suspicious for sure, so I continue to stroll through the cart pod, but very slowly, and never moving too far from Greg's Grilled Cheese. I need to see what Shaggy and Scarface order. It could be important. It could lead to another clue.

I decide to skim the menu boards for the word *whiskey*. Most food carts can't serve alcohol, so maybe whiskey is a flavoring or maybe just a word in the food dish's title. As I start to read the menu at the Noodle Nub, a dog begins barking frantically. It's coming from just outside the pod on the sidewalk. Peering through a gap between two carts, I see that the dog belongs to a man sitting on the sidewalk, leaning against a telephone pole. He's homeless, I'm pretty certain. He holds tightly to the leash of the barking mutt.

I feel a strange tug pulling me toward this man and his dog. The mutt looks so scroungy. He could use some grub. There's probably plenty of food scraps in the garbage here. I step to a bin nearby and peer over the rim, but then quickly stop.

What am I doing?

This is something Hank and Coral would be doing.

I back away from the garbage when the unbelievable happens again.

He happens again.

Joey Marino.

He's suddenly standing next to the homeless man. He must be the person the dog's barking at. Joey reaches his hand toward the dog's nose, his palm down. The dog sniffs and stops barking. Joey crouches down and hands something to the man. It's something in a wrapper, like a granola bar, and then he yanks off his backpack and pulls out . . . his phone. He holds it out next to the homeless man. They stare at the phone together. I can't see their expressions.

This is the second time I've seen Joey talking with homeless people.

What is up with him?

What is he sharing on his phone with them?

What are they talking about?

I shake my head because why does it matter?

I make my way back to Greg's Grilled Cheese. Shaggy and Scarface are nowhere in sight.

I almost curse aloud.

I've lost a possible lead to a clue.

And it's all Joey Marino's fault.

Chapter Twelve

Willa's House

"Poppy, be nice." I turn my palm down in front of Hank's newest chicken the next morning.

"I'm going to reach underneath you and grab . . . OUCH!" I jerk my hand back and shake it vigorously. "You just skewered me with your beak!" A bead of blood appears on the lower knuckle of my thumb.

"Fine. Keep your egg. Good luck getting it to hatch." And then under my breath, I say, "Stupid fowl."

I return to the kitchen to rinse my stab wound in the sink, when Coral saunters in completely topless.

"Coral! Can you put a shirt on already?" I blurt.

"Oh, MacKenna, I'm going outside to get one." She waves her hand at me. "I forgot to bring my laundry in from the line last night." She walks straight out to the backyard, skin glowing in the morning sun.

My little flipper vibrates in my pocket. It's a text from

Willa: I can help hunt today. Meet at my house at 10:30.

This is fantastic news. Yesterday was a complete bust, and now there are only seven days to find eight clues, and we're no closer to solving the second riddle.

I'm rummaging through the pantry to find one of Coral's homemade granola bars when she comes back inside, pulling a T-shirt over her head.

"Are you going somewhere?" Coral asks.

"I'm meeting Willa at her house. Food cart research, remember?"

"Oh, of course." She kisses my cheek. "Well, don't be too late, honey. Hank and Coho will need help with the fence this afternoon! Tomorrow's the big reveal day."

I don't ask what she means. I don't want to know.

I briskly walk the half mile or so to Willa's house, my stomach growling. Maybe Willa's mom will make me some waffles. One day, when I'm a computer programmer, I'll own a home like Willa's. Four bedrooms, three bathrooms, remodeled kitchen, large-screen TV in the family room. There'll be no hens in the garage, only cars, maybe two. There'll be a sprinkler system to keep the lawn green, ceramic pots filled with flowers bought from the grocery store nursery, and absolutely no plants surrounded with smelly organic compost.

I step onto the porch and ring the doorbell. Several moments later, Willa's mom answers. Her face is blotchy, and her eyes are red and watery.

"Oh, Mac. I think Willa should be home soon." She wipes her eyes and doesn't invite me inside like usual. "How about you wait on the porch."

"Okay. Sure."

Willa's mom manages to half smile before closing the door. I sit on the porch swing. Weird. I thought Willa was home. Where is she? What's wrong with her mom?

A few moments later, a seafoam-green sedan pulls into the driveway. It's Willa's dad. Willa and her sister, Becca, hop out of the car. They both have their backpacks, which is sort of odd. Willa's dad waves at them from his open window, then he backs out of the driveway and takes off.

Becca bops onto the front porch and gives me a fist bump and a hip bump. "Hi, Mac." She pushes the front door open and goes inside. "Mom!"

"Hey." Willa drops her backpack on the porch.

"Hey, yourself." I want to ask what's going on, where she's been, what's wrong with her mom, but Brie arrives before the questions can pour from my lips.

Willa smiles when she sees Brie. "How'd you do?"

"First in the two hundred 'fly, second in the two hundred individual medley, and we won the four hundred medley relay," Brie recites. She smiles at us, but it looks fake. She doesn't seem happy with her results.

"That brings out the swim moves in me!" Willa

backstrokes her arms and swivels her hips. Her blond curls flow side to side.

"What about you? Did you get another clue yesterday?" Willa plops down on the swing next to me.

"Hardly." I proceed to tell them about going to the Division Street carts, about seeing Shaggy and Scarface and then losing them before I could see what they ordered at Greg's Grilled Cheese.

"Jack cheese, huh?" Brie says. "Maybe we should go there and get some sandwiches and see what happens."

"I thought about that, but we need to be certain, so we don't waste money."

"True," Brie says.

"I also saw Joey again. He was talking to a homeless man, showing the man something on his phone."

"What's with him and all the homeless friends?" Willa asks.

"Maybe he volunteers at a shelter or soup kitchen or something," Brie says. "It wouldn't surprise me, especially now that we know he did all that stuff at school."

"Hey!" Willa jumps off the swing and claps her hands. "Forget about Joey. Are we solving this clue today?"

"I only have until two," Brie answers. "I had to beg my parents to let me out of the house this morning. They wanted me to stay home and rest and ice my shoulder."

"What's wrong with your fin?" Willa asks. We watch

Brie slowly roll her right shoulder forward and back.

"I don't know. It's just a little sore," she says. "It'll be fine. I have a light workout this evening."

Willa snaps her fingers. "Hey, my dad eats at this burrito cart downtown. It's probably not the cart we need, but we could head down there and do some clue hunting."

"Great," I say.

"Let's do a treasure hunt dance before we go, some ballet, I think." Willa gets off the swing, raises herself onto her toes, and reaches her hands over her head. "Be careful with your shoulder, Brie. Come on, Mac, on your tippy-toes."

Chapter Thirteen

The Alder Street Carts

Willa convinces her mom to give us a ride downtown. She drops us off at the corner of Alder and 4th Avenue. We walk down the sidewalk, weaving between all the people waiting in line for their cart fare of the day. There are colorful trailers around the entire city block, smashed together so tightly, you can barely fit a pencil through the gaps.

I smell spicy curry. Five steps later, I inhale the sugary molasses scent of barbecue. Five more steps and it's sizzling bacon. I could eat at these carts every single day of my life if I had the money. No more kale and homemade granola for me.

We pass a Japanese cart and I stop. Standing there, glancing at the menu, are Shaggy and Scarface.

"That's them!" I say quietly to Willa and Brie. "The two I told you about. They're in this hunt."

"I hope that's not a cart we need. I don't like sushi," Willa said.

"I love it," Brie admits, "but I don't think that's the right cart for our clue. Maybe for a future clue?"

"Maybe." I make a mental note of the cart name, Sho's Sushi. I'll be sure to add it to my notes.

"Should we follow them?" Willa asks.

I shake my head. "Don't let them see us. They might recognize me. We're safer keeping a distance."

"Hey," Willa says, "look at that couple by the slider place. They're looking at a napkin. I bet it's a clue."

"How many people do you think know about this hunt?" Brie asks.

"More than I'd like there to be. Come on, let's get closer," I say. "Maybe they just got the clue at that slider cart."

We creep through the sidewalk crowd toward the napkin couple.

"I could totally snatch it from them," Willa whispers. "I could just skip up to them, stumble, and bump right into them."

"That's cheating, Willa," Brie says.

I know Brie's right, but it's still tempting to see that napkin.

We linger near the couple until the woman tucks the napkin into her purse.

I sigh and gaze at the menu at the slider cart. Nothing stands out to me. There's no mention of whiskey, or pads, or anything that seems like it would relate to the second clue.

I've been working on this riddle for over forty-eight hours now. I really need to solve it today to stay on my timeline.

"'Put a tag in early, then pull up a pad,'" I recite. "I can't decode that line." I turn around and kick a nearby garbage can.

"Relax, Mac," Brie says. "Let's keep checking out these carts. There's a lot of them."

We pass a pasta cart, scan the menu, and quickly rule it out. Next is a juice cart. That isn't right either. I completely lose track of Shaggy and Scarface and the napkin team, which probably means that there's no clue at any of these carts. I check my watch. The clock is ticking. Our chances at solving this clue are dwindling.

The last cart on the block is a place called Oasis. It has a clear plastic awning with a hanging lantern. Willa, Brie, and I step closer and check out the menu. Instead of a board listing their menu, this place has colored photos for every dish served. The smell lures me, the garlic, the onions and tomatoes.

"Look." Brie points to a very small wooden deck attached to the side of the cart. "They don't have a table, but they have pillows to sit on."

And sure enough, about four people are sitting on cushions right on the tiny patio.

"Maybe those are the pads from the clue," Willa says.

I feel my eye sockets bulge. "Willa! Yes!" And then in a softer voice, I say, "'Pull up a pad.' This could be it. Let's look at those pictures again."

We move back under the awning to study the food pictures. Willa reads aloud and points at each one. "Moroccan couscous, Casablanca cheesesteak sandwich." She pauses. "Oh, that sounds amazing."

Brie takes over reading the menu. "Seafood paella, kefta tagine, Moroccan lamb sandwich—"

"Stop. Look." I reach toward the photo of the kefta tagine and put my finger right on the title. "I think this is it!"

"What?" Willa says. "How do you know?"

"It's the word *tagine*. It's in our clue." I reach into my shoulder bag and pull out the cup sleeve from my hunt folder. "Put a *tag in early*. Do you see it?"

I must be talking loudly because a few heads nearby turn, and Brie hushes me with a finger to her lips. I point again to the word and mouth, "*Tag, in,* and the *e* in early."

Willa and Brie stare at the word and then at me, grins growing on their faces.

"You are a riddle superstar, Mac! Those clue tricksters don't fool you," Willa says. "Let's go order."

"Wait. Let me borrow your phone," I say.

Willa powers it up and hands it over to me, and I do a quick search of *Morocco* and *whiskey*. "Listen to this." I'm smiling as I read aloud from the article I've found. "'Mint tea is everywhere in Morocco. It's commonly referred to as Moroccan whiskey.'"

"Genius!" Willa pumps her fist. We all high-five once and then step in line to order.

"I'll have a Kefta Tagine," I say, likely pronouncing it wrong. I note the cost: eight dollars.

"And a mint tea," Brie pipes in.

That's two more dollars. Three dollars and thirty-three cents for each of us.

"And a Casablanca cheesesteak sandwich!" Willa shouts.

"What? That's an extra nine dollars."

"Don't worry. It's on me. I can't resist." She does a quick pirouette.

I pull out my notes and write down the food costs, subtracting it from my savings. The woman in the Oasis trailer looks annoyed when I lay out all my coins on the counter, but she sweeps them into her palm along with Willa's and Brie's bills. After a few minutes of waiting, the woman hands us a cup of steaming tea, a paper tray with Willa's cheesesteak sandwich, and finally a pie tin filled with stew-like deliciousness of meatballs, tomatoes, olives, eggs, and cheeses. The cushions on the little wooden patio are open now, so we all *pull up a pad* and sit down, setting the food between us.

I gently pull out the napkin from under the tin of kefta tagine. It has writing on it:

Does your head ache, or is it your feet?
The sunshine tropics will be felt in your seat.

Chapter Fourteen

Where Cold Drinks Are Needed

Thirty minutes ago, I was kicking garbage cans and seriously considering swiping clues out of others' hands. But now, we have three clues, and I feel like screaming *Victory!*

"I know this!" I jump off the pad. "I've already solved this clue."

"What?" Brie says.

"You guys, this is the smoothie cart. You know, the man who pedals around town, and then he stops, and you can get on his bike and blend your own smoothie?"

Brie gasps. "Pedal with your *feet*. Feel it in your *seat*."

"Yes," I say.

Willa grabs the napkin from me and reads it carefully. "How do you feel sunshine tropics in your seat? That sounds uncomfortable."

"I think Sunshine Tropics is the name of the smoothie we order." I throw my arms in the air. "Willa, we should be doing your hunt dance! I can't believe this. It's almost too easy. And guess what?" I don't wait for their responses. "I saw this guy when we passed Pioneer Courthouse Square on our way here. He was set up right on the bricks. That's like five blocks away."

I stoop down and grab the tagine pie tin to throw it away. I'm ready to roll. There's another clue within our grasp, and finding it will put us right back on track. I give myself a moment to imagine what I might create at coding camp, maybe a food cart app. One that helps you locate just the right cart in the city, depending on your hunger and location.

But then Brie shrieks. "You guys! It's almost one. I have to be home by two." She pulls out her phone. "My mom is going to freak. I thought we'd be back on the east side by now."

"I'll call my mom," Willa says, handing me back the napkin with the clue. "She'll come get us."

"Wait," I say. "The square is so close. We could have another clue in about thirty minutes. I really saw this smoothie cart."

But my friends don't seem to be listening or sharing any of the excitement that this clue has brought me. Can't they see my skin is practically splitting open?

Brie fidgets. She rubs her shoulder. She checks her phone for messages.

Willa texts her mom. I know she'll come. She always does.

My team is abandoning me.

Like yesterday.

I'll have to move forward on my own.

Like yesterday.

Willa and Brie catch their ride, and I walk alone to Pioneer Courthouse Square, a big city block lined with red brick. Kids, musicians, and homeless people stroll around the square, and I think of Joey Marino, wondering if he's here, looking for clues like me. I search the bricks, combing the groups of people, but I don't see Joey anywhere.

The bigger problem is that I don't see the smoothie guy either.

Don't panic, I tell myself, trying to sound soothing like Brie. Everything's okay. That's what Willa would say.

I make my way around the square, past the Starbucks, the benches, the MAX train stops. I look across the streets, and head back to the corner where I was certain the smoothie guy was set up earlier.

Where did he go? Did I just imagine seeing him?

I spy an old city worker sweeping sidewalk trash. His wrinkly hands hold the push broom tightly, and his back has a permanent hump, probably from all the years of leaning over.

"Excuse me, sir?" I approach him. "I'm looking for a little food cart. It's a guy with a bicycle and very small trailer. He sells smoothies?"

The old man looks at me, and then peers up the block to where I stood just a few seconds ago. "He's already gone." The man's voice crackles.

"What do you mean he's already gone?"

"Well," the old man says, leaning on his broom. "He's here one moment, gone the next. Can't count on those moving carts to stay in one place for too long."

"Where would he have gone?" I ask.

"I couldn't begin to tell you." The old man pauses. "I suppose he goes wherever the cold drinks are needed." Then he stoops over and continues his sidewalk sweeping.

Wherever the cold drinks are needed.

That doesn't exactly narrow things down.

I make a mental list of such places: parks, swimming pools, baseball and soccer fields, tracks . . .

I happen to know from Coral that there are over two hundred parks in the city of Portland, nestled in neighborhoods in every section of town. Some stretch for endless, grassy, cool-drink-needing miles.

I plop down on a bench and let out a deep exhale.

This search is more challenging than any robotics project or computer code I've ever tried writing. Just when I think I'm getting close and putting all the steps in the right order, the program stops and a message pops up: LOGIC ERROR.

This will take more troubleshooting than I've ever done before.

Girls Are Supercoders.

Right now, that poster's a lie, at least when it comes to me.

I need better powers, and I'm not sure how to get them.

Chapter Fifteen

More New Housemates

When I open my eyes on Monday morning, the first thing I see is Coral, already up, drinking her green tea across the living room. Seeing her there on the futon couch makes me think of when I was little, when she would wait for me to wake up. She'd beam her morning smile at me, and I'd crawl off my floor futon and into her lap, where I'd sniff her green-tea-and-flax smell. She'd sing me her corny songs about saving the earth and planting gardens, and I'd sing with her, giggling when she'd break into her animal chirpings and howls. But that was before I knew about naked bike riding, and drumming circles, and laughter therapy. Before I became Bongo Girl and Kalebrains and discovered all the things I was missing, the things that most kids my age had, like TVs in their homes and their own bedrooms and cars to ride in and computers.

"MacKenna! You're awake. Today's such a big day. Don't

worry about the chickens and eggs, Hank and Coho got up very early, and they handled it."

I don't like the way she's looking at me, with that eyebrow-to-eyebrow grin on her face, like she really might burst into a Save-the-Earth song. "What's going on?"

"It's our summer plan reveal day. You're going to be so surprised."

I rub my eyes. I didn't sleep well last night. All I could think about was that there are six days left to find seven clues. That's approximately twenty hours per clue. My only focus for today is finding the smoothie cart so I can get the fourth clue.

"I really don't want to be surprised. Please just tell me."

"I can't. I promised Hank. They should be back in less than an hour." Coral continues to smile at me and sip her tea. "Let's converse about your research. Tell me how it's going." She pats the futon, inviting me to sit next to her.

I straighten my bedsheets, pulling them tight. Coral is cramping my morning routine, but I ask, "Have you ever seen that guy who has the moving smoothie cart? He rides his bike around with the trailer and stops to sell the smoothies?"

"Yes, I have. It's a fantastic environmentally sound business model, don't you think?"

"I guess so." I reach into my dresser basket for clean clothes. "I'm trying to find him today."

"I have a friend in my bicycling club who knows him," Coral says.

The shirt falls from my hand. "You do?"

Coral nods.

"Do you think your friend knows the smoothie guy's schedule, like where he sets up his cart every day?"

Coral looks at me carefully, probably sizing up my rare enthusiasm. "I'll see Marshaun on Saturday at the big bike ride. I can ask."

Saturday?

I can't wait that long. The hunt ends on Saturday. I need to find Smoothie Guy immediately, preferably in the next twenty hours.

"Can you call or text him and ask today?"

"Oh. I suppose, but I don't know where I put my phone."

I get up and go into the bathroom, and return with Coral's phone, flipping it open and holding it out to her.

"You're serious about your research, aren't you?"

"Very."

"Hank and I are so proud of your community spirit. You're becoming just like that wonderful Joey Marino." Coral stands up and hugs me.

A bubble of air lodges in my lungs. Coral's not hugging me, the real Mac. Once again, she's hugging who she wants me to be. This hunt has nothing to do with Hank and Coral's community spirit. I glance at my coding poster above my island. *Girls Are Supercoders*. That's *my* community spirit. That's why I'm doing this hunt.

I pull out of her arms. "So, you'll ask your friend today about the smoothie guy?"

"Yes."

I return to the bathroom to dress and braid my hair when I hear Hank's voice. "Coral, Mac! Come outside! They're here."

Coral lets out a squeal. I finish tying the hair band at the end of my braid, and I walk warily through the kitchen and out into the backyard where I see . . .

"GOATS!"

Coral throws her hands up and dashes toward one of the creatures, but it darts away from her, jumping in little circles.

"Whoa," Coho says. "We all need to be chill right now while these little nannies acclimate."

"Oh, Hank, Coho, they are so cute." Coral claps her hands.

"What are you thinking?" I back up toward the kitchen door.

"Goat yoga. That's what we're thinking. It's our new addition to the festival this year," Hank answers. "Coho helped us get these beauties. He met a farmer just out on Foster Road where his new land is, and we biked out and picked them up this morning. All three fit in our bike trailers plus a bail of timothy hay."

Coral inches toward one of the goats. It's brownish with some white patches around its face. "See why we needed the fence, MacKenna? We can't have these precious girls eating my vegetables." She reaches a hand out slowly and touches the animal's back.

"You. Can't. Have. Goats," I say. "We don't live on a farm. We don't even live in the country. This is an inner-city neighborhood. There. Are. Restrictions."

"Mac." Hank moves toward me and sets his hands on my shoulders, attempting to calm me down. "We're only keeping them for two weeks. One week to get to know us all, and one week for the festival."

"But . . . do you even know anything about goats?"

"Coho knows a little," Hank says.

"He does?"

What could a former information technology professional possibly know about goats?

"These are Nigerian Dwarf goats," Coho states. He points to the brown animal that Coral is now petting and kissing on the ears. "That's Ziggy, and the other brown one is Marley. The gray one with the white belly patches is Emmylou. They're all just over a year old."

"Goat yoga is popular now," Hank says. "I've been dying to try it."

"It's weird," I add. "No. It's worse than weird because

you're breaking city rules!" A scream wells up inside my chest like a balloon about to burst.

"They say goats enhance your yoga experience," Coho says. "Their presence and natural curiosity emits a calm energy, allowing you to hold the asanas and breathe."

"They could pee on you! That's gross."

Emmylou hops up onto a lawn chair and then pops right onto Coral's planting table against the side of the house. The Ziggy-Marley twins bounce over to me, but I back away. I will not pet these goats. I don't want them here. They shouldn't be here at all.

"I'm not taking care of them," I say. Ziggy and Marley continue to pursue me. I'm walking in circles to keep them away.

Emmylou jumps off the table, knocking three of Coral's pots onto the grass. The terra-cotta breaks into pieces, but Emmylou just prances toward Ziggy and Marley, and they all tail me now.

"They like you, Mac," Coho says. "See how naturally curious they are?"

"Well, I don't like them or their natural curiosity." I stretch out my palms, frantically attempting to push them away.

"They perceive your energy. Use eye blinking to calm them," Coho tells me.

"What are you talking about?!"

"Eye blinking, Mac," Coho instructs again. He steps toward me and quietly squats down near the trio of goats. Emmylou drops some poop pellets right in the middle of the lawn.

Gross!

"I'm not taking care of them," I repeat. "I have my food cart research, remember?"

I spin away and open the back door to escape to my island.

If only I could completely escape.

Chapter Sixteen

Never Enough Money

I flop down on my belly, my face into my pillow.

Yoga goats.

Brie would tell me to relax and brush it off.

Willa would tell me to stand up and dance because dancing makes everything better.

They have no idea.

I can't just dance away or brush off Hank and Coral's weirdness. It won't ever go away. What will my classmates think now? I'll be Goat Girl . . . or worse.

I bang my forehead into my pillow again and again.

"MacKenna?" Coral whispers. "We should have asked you first about the goats. Hank and I are remorseful for that, but we're hopeful that you'll bond with them."

She speaks sincerely, but I keep my face on my pillow and don't answer or forgive.

"Well, I'm going to help spread some of the hay for

them, but I want you to know that I heard back from my friend Marshaun. He told me his smoothie cart friend is going to be at the zoo today."

I lift my head and see Coral wave before she leaves the living room.

The smoothie cart is at the zoo! That means the fourth clue is at the zoo!

I tap out a text to Willa and Brie right away.

Brie responds first: Got a doctor's appointment after swim practice. Maybe tomorrow.

I can't wait until tomorrow. Smoothie Guy won't be at the zoo tomorrow.

A few minutes later, my phone buzzes again. It's Willa: Can't today. Stuff is happening.

What stuff could be happening? What good are team-mates if they never show up for the big game?

I'll just have to go on my own. I'll bus downtown to the MAX station and take the train to the zoo. I pull out my hunt folder, looking at my three clues. Without Willa and Brie, I'll have to pay for the smoothie on my own. I don't know how much it will cost. Maybe five dollars? Maybe as much as eight dollars. After sharing the tagine, I only have $11.10 left.

And then I realize something else. I'm going to have to pay for admission to the zoo to get this clue.

That's twelve dollars and ninety-five cents!

Why do things have to cost so much?

I head back to the kitchen to find some breakfast, hoping food will give me ideas. The morning eggs are still on the counter in the basket, so I put them in the refrigerator and grab the carton of soy milk.

Out the window, I watch my parents and Coho and the three new housemates. All the goats are now standing on Coral's planting table. Coho's trying to coax the animals down, probably with his eye blinking, but Ziggy and Marley and Emmylou don't seem to want to move anymore.

They can stay on top of that table the whole two weeks as far as I'm concerned.

Coho's duffel bag sits on top of the kitchen table, unzipped with a couple of shirts hanging out. I shove it aside to make room for my breakfast when I see a wallet.

I stare at it. Thinking. Wondering.

Outside, Hank drops the hay bale next to the new fence they built. The goats are still on Coral's table.

I look at the wallet again . . . and touch it. It's old leather and very soft.

Outside Coho's back is turned. He's helping Hank rake the hay now, spreading it over the grass.

I pull his wallet out of his bag and open it, slowly. There's a library card, a couple of credit cards, and a driver's license for the state of California. And tucked in the length of the wallet are some bills. Lots of bills. Sifting through them,

I count six ones, three fives, three tens, and two twenties. Ninety-one dollars touching my fingertips. No coins, just crisp, green, American bills.

No. This is wrong.

I shouldn't be touching this.

I toss the wallet back in his bag and look out the window again.

Coho continues to rake. The bale of hay grows smaller as he spreads it out across the grass. I was counting on cousin James, I mean Coho, to help me. He was supposed to be my ticket to the computer camp, my ticket to becoming a supercoder. But he's nothing like he used to be. He brought us a mean, hand-stabbing, Rhode Island Red chicken. He goes biking naked with Coral. He sleeps in their bed, eats our food, plays his guitar, sings horribly, and now he brings in three yoga goats.

Doesn't he owe us for our hospitality?

I grab the wallet again and count his bills. It would be so easy to slip a few out. I wonder if he even knows exactly how much he has.

I slide out one ten and three ones, then tuck the others back neatly.

Thirteen dollars right here in my palm.

This is so wrong.

So wrong.

So wrong.

But, yet . . . it's only thirteen dollars. It's not like I'm taking *all* his money. It's kind of just a tiny loan to get me by, just so I can enter the zoo. I'm going to use *my* coins to buy the smoothie, to receive the next clue, to continue the hunt, to find the remaining clues, to win the grand prize, to go to computer camp, to . . . be a supercoder.

I fold Coho's bills and shove them into my pocket.

This is wrong, wrong, wrong.

But I'll pay the goat man back, after I win.

I will.

Chapter Seventeen

The Bus Ride

By the time I hop on the bus to head downtown it's nearly ten in the morning. I find a seat near the back and fold my shoulder bag with my hunt folder, coins, and flipper phone on my lap. I reach into the front pocket of my jeans for about the hundredth time to assure myself that I still have the thirteen dollars I stole to get into the zoo. Coho's money gnaws on my mind—have I turned into *Hippie Thief Chick*? I keep reminding myself that I'll pay it back, just as soon as I win the prize money. I only need five hundred dollars for coding camp. I'll have plenty to spare.

I close my eyes and try to focus on the hunt and the clues, not the stolen money or the goats or any of the other daily weirdness.

I sense motion next to me as someone sits down, but my eyes stay closed, still attempting to focus.

Three clues. The fourth to come. Six to go.

Coho won't notice the money missing. Will he?

Does your head ache, or is it your feet?

If Coho does notice, will he say anything to Hank and Coral?

The sunshine tropics will be felt in your seat.

The next clue is so close.

The bus brakes squeal as it slows for a stop. My eyes open and, "AHH!" I startle, slapping my hands onto my bag so it doesn't fall to the bus floor.

Sitting at my side is Joey Marino.

"Sorry!" Joey scoots away from me just a smidge. "I—I didn't mean to scare you."

I pull my bag into my belly. "What are you doing here?"

Joey doesn't answer me right away. He fidgets and swallows. "Um . . . I'm riding the bus?"

Uh-huh. Right. I happen to know that the statistical probability of running into the exact same person three times in four days in a city of more than six hundred thousand people is extremely low.

I clutch my shoulder bag. "Where are you going?"

Joey clears his throat. "Downtown."

The sound of his voice surprises me again, the lowness, the softness.

"Where are you going?" he asks.

"To the—" But I stop myself before revealing the truth, because Joey is in this hunt too. He has at least two clues.

He's my competition. I should be careful.

"Downtown," I say.

He just nods.

The bus rumbles over the Hawthorne Bridge.

Joey begins pulling items out of his backpack, and I observe his every move, pretending to be looking straight ahead. First, he takes out a granola bar, then a bottle of water, then a brown wool scarf, which he rolls into a tidy spiral. He grabs some change, appears to count it (three dollars in quarters, I quickly calculate), then slips the coins into a side pocket. He reaches deep into the pack and pulls out more quarters (five, I think). His backpack is seemingly bottomless. He takes out a T-shirt and folds it, then a paperback book called *The Bluest Eye*, and finally some more coins, dimes and nickels.

The bus squeals to a stop at 6th and Main just as every item is returned to Joey's pack.

I stand, and Joey rises, letting me pass, then he gets off the bus after me.

I make my way down the street toward Pioneer Place and the MAX train stop that will take me out to the zoo. I don't look to see if Joey is following me, but I sense that he is.

Two blocks later, I'm in front of the stop.

Joey is too.

There's a teen leaning against a trash can. Her hair falls across her face. Her arm has a tattoo of an alligator with a tail that wraps around her bicep. I wonder if she's homeless.

Joey and the teen make eye contact. The teen motions with her head across 5th Avenue. Joey looks in that direction, and then he crosses the street.

I start to move too, but I catch myself and stop. What am I doing? I'm not following Joey Marino.

All I'm doing is waiting for the train.

To go to the zoo. To find the smoothie cart. To get the next clue.

But I can't help watching him.

He walks toward someone who's leaning against the brick wall of a bank. It's a woman in a heavy wool jacket. Her head is hunched over, and she seems to be quivering, looking in all directions, like every movement catches her attention for nanoseconds of time.

Joey steps closer to her. I step closer to the edge of the sidewalk to see better.

Joey approaches the woman with a hand stretched forward. It seems like he says something to her, then he reaches into his backpack and hands her the book, *The Bluest Eye*.

He's a—a librarian for the homeless? Is this his newest community project? Coral would eat this up.

Then, surprisingly, the woman reaches for Joey and grabs his shoulders, pulling him toward her. Joey's arms flare out, like he's startled, like I would be if some strange person suddenly grabbed me.

Is he okay? My heartbeat sprints. Should I do something?

Without another thought, I bolt across 5th Avenue, ignoring the Do Not Cross sign, knowing there's just enough time before the lines of traffic move.

"Joey!" I yell, paying no attention to the fact that his hands are now touching the woman's coat.

Joey flinches when he hears my voice. I'm only four feet from him now. The woman still holds his shoulders.

"Hey!" I holler again. "Let him go!"

The woman lets Joey go, but she looks piercingly at me, and I shiver.

I can't read her eyes, but I see that they're stonelike gray.

And then the woman spins and flees down 5th Avenue, the book in her hand, her old heavy wool jacket flapping behind her. People on the sidewalk shift out of her way.

Joey takes a couple of steps, like he's about to follow the woman, but then he reels around toward me. "Mac!" He stomps his combat boot on the sidewalk.

"I—"

"I was talking to her!" He crosses his arms tightly, glaring at me.

"I didn't know." I pant. I'm no longer shivering. Now I'm sweating.

The Walk sign flashes and Joey soldiers across the street. I follow him.

"You should be more careful around the street people," I say.

"The street people?" He leans toward me. "You say that like they're rats."

"That's not what I meant," I stammer.

"You don't know what you're talking about. They're human beings, Mac. Like you and me."

"Sorry," I say, but it's barely a whisper, and I'm not sure if Joey even hears me.

The MAX train slides forward and stops. The doors whoosh open.

"Is this your train?" Joey's voice is icy.

"Yeah." I step on and grab a handrail.

A few moments later, Joey gets on too. He passes me without a glance and steps to the upper section, sitting down next to a man who's staring at his phone.

The train inches forward, and the MAX voice announces the next stop, first in English, then in Spanish.

Carefully, I creep to the upper section and sit down across the aisle from Joey. He just gazes ahead.

"Do you know that woman?" I finally ask.

Joey clutches his backpack. His combat boots are glued to the floor of the train.

"Sometimes," he answers.

Chapter Eighteen

The Smoothie Cart

Joey and I are silent the whole rumbling train ride, and the silence is *thick*. It presses on me, squeezing across my chest like a coat that's two sizes too small. I have so many questions for Joey, like what he was doing talking to that woman and why did he give her a book? But I also want to ask why he's on this MAX train when he said he was going downtown. Is he following me? Does he think I will lead him to the next clue?

There's no point in asking because the one thing I do know about Joey Marino is that he's not much of a talker.

I try to focus on the smoothie cart and getting the next clue. I remind myself again that Joey's my competition.

I get off the train at the zoo exit. Joey steps off right behind me. We both make our way out of the tunnel to the entrance. I find the shortest ticket line, and hand the clerk Coho's thirteen dollars for admission, tucking my nickel change into my shoulder bag. Joey's no longer near me, but I spy him at the Members Only line.

Keeping a keen eye on Joey, I step behind a group of people. Thankfully, it's summer and the zoo's busy. Little kids are running all over the place, dropping popcorn kernels on the pavement. Maybe I can be as stealthy and quiet as Joey is. Maybe I'll blend into the crowd like he always manages to do.

Staying behind the group, I walk down the long pathway that leads to the animal exhibits. I'm not positive where the smoothie cart will be set up, so I pay close attention to all the little kiosks, always keeping Joey in my line of vision. He's walking ahead of me now, very slowly. Too slowly. The group providing my camouflage passes him, but I hold back.

Then Joey turns around and spies me before I can duck out of the way. I speed up my pace to get in front of him. I pass a monkey exhibit and see a women's bathroom ahead. Slipping through the door, I exhale. I'll just wait here a bit while Joey moves on.

After a full five minutes, I peek out the doorway.

Joey Marino's not around, but I double-check to be sure. One thing I've learned is just because I can't see this boy, it doesn't mean he isn't there.

My best guess is that Smoothie Guy will be near the grassy amphitheater where they have bird shows and summer music concerts. I move along the path in that direction, sneaking constant glances all over. As I near the amphithe-ater, I see five food carts, and I can't hold back my grin when I see Smoothie Guy's bicycle trailer. He stands under a tall umbrella near a fold-up table covered with cups, spoons, and napkins. I'm buzzing with my good fortune and the nearness of my next clue, and the prize money, and my com-puter camp. I rub my palms together. It's like I've executed a perfect computer program.

Smoothie Guy has his bicycle up on a stand to make it stationary, like an exercise bike. On the handle bars is a blender, rigged so that the blades rotate when the pedals of the bike turn.

There's a line of three people waiting to pedal their smoothies. I join them.

The woman at the front of the line orders a Strawberry Sensation smoothie and sits down on the bike seat. I watch her pedal while the clue churns in my head. *Does your head ache, or is it your feet? The sunshine tropics will be felt in your seat.*

There's only two sizes of smoothies, regular and large. I figure I need to order large. It's seven dollars. I open my bag and begin to pull out quarters and dimes, shoving them in my jeans pocket as I count.

"What kind are you getting?"

Poof! Joey Marino stands right beside me.

Again.

How does he always find me? And what am I supposed to do? I can't get out of line and then come back. This computer program glitch is unexpected.

"I haven't decided yet," I lie.

"I'm thinking Paradise Beach," he says.

I puzzle this, wondering whether Joey even has the clue for this cart. Maybe he's trying to steer me in the wrong direction, or maybe he knows something I don't know. I need to play this cautiously.

"Next!" Smoothie Guy hollers, wiping a clean blender container.

I step forward and whisper, "Large Sunshine Tropics."

Smoothie Guy nods, a slight smile on his lips.

I peek over my shoulder. Joey Marino's still there, but I don't think he heard my order. I position myself directly in front of Smoothie Guy to block Joey's view so he can't see what ingredients are being added to the container.

When it's filled, Smoothie Guy steps to the bicycle and attaches the container to the blender base on the handlebars. "Start pedaling."

I climb on and pedal. Joey watches me the whole time, his gray eyes dulling. And that's when I know for sure. He doesn't have this clue. He's been following me in hopes of finding this clue and then another. I study the menu choices as I pedal. Joey has a one-in-ten chance of guessing the correct smoothie.

I pedal faster until Smoothie Guy tells me to stop and get off. He unlatches the container and pours the fruit smoothie into a tall paper cup. A rush of satisfaction flows through my body.

Smoothie Guy hands me the cup. "Enjoy. Next!"

Joey steps forward without looking at me and says, "I'll have what she ordered."

I'm not sure how, but I refrain from screaming out loud. I sprint out of the amphitheater area. My lungs heave as I race up the hill to the exit. Now Joey Marino has another clue too. How is it possible for me to be so stupid and so unlucky? Now I know his game. He's stalking me to get the hunt clues.

It's not until I get on the MAX train that I unfold the napkin around the smoothie cup. Written in red ink is my fourth clue:

Green, gold, and purple spices might get your arm strong.
Shrimpy legs don't let you dance, but you can sing a song.

Chapter Nineteen

Brie's Crisis

The blankets on the futon across the room are in a heap when I wake up the following morning, and Hank and Coral aren't there. I smell incense burning, the signal that they're practicing yoga.

Today I have no seconds to waste. I need to meet up with Willa and Brie right away. We have some serious thinking and researching to do on the fourth clue.

As soon as I finish my hair, Willa texts me: My house. 9 a.m. Brie has a crisis.

I respond: What's wrong?

But Willa doesn't text back.

I click my flipper shut. In the kitchen I unhook the egg basket and head outside.

Hank, Coral, Coho, and two women I recognize from Hank's drumming circle are all in downward dog on yoga mats in the backyard. Hank calmly gives directions. Ziggy,

Marley, and Emmylou stand on Coral's gardening table, watching them all.

I laugh to myself. Even the goats think goat yoga is weird. They want nothing to do with it. So much for enhancing the experience.

Inside the garage coop, Poppy sits in her nesting box, her eyes glowing at me. I sense another morning battle brewing, and my arm muscles tense. I'll try quickness instead of slyness today. I shove my hand under her belly, feeling the warm egg. Just as I yank it out, she snaps her head down, pecking me sharply on the wrist.

"You are not a nice chicken." I point my finger at her. "You're an illegal intruder. Just like those goats."

I grab the eggs left by the leghorns and return to the kitchen. I'm not hungry for Coral's dry muffins, so I pack my bag and set out to Willa's house.

She's sitting on the porch swing, her head down, staring at her phone, when I arrive, but she jumps up when she sees me. "Bad news. Brie has a shoulder sprain."

For most people, this wouldn't be a crisis of life proportions, but to Brie Vo and her parents, this is as close to near death as a person could get.

"No swimming for six weeks," Willa says.

"Dang."

Poor Brie.

"She's a mess. We should go see her."

"Yeah," I say, "of course."

As we walk, I talk nonstop and tell Willa all about yesterday, starting with the new goats and then the bus ride and Joey Marino and how he gave a book to this homeless woman, and then how I got the clue at the smoothie food cart.

Willa doesn't respond at all, not even about the goats, which I figured would make her dance or at least laugh, but there's no skip or twirl in her step today.

"Willa? Are you okay? You're really quiet."

"Just thinking about a lot of stuff that's going on at my house."

"Is it about the other day? Is your mom okay?"

We're right in front of Brie's house now, and Willa says, "I'll tell you later. Let's go see Brie."

We knock on the front door, and Mrs. Vo lets us in. The lights are dimmed, and Brie is on the couch, flat on her back. Her silky black hair drapes neatly over her chest. Her eyes are closed, and her hands clasp together on her belly. It feels like we're entering a funeral. The whole scene kind of creeps me out until Mrs. Vo brings in a plate of milk cakes, which Brie's dad likely made.

Sugar deliciousness goes a long way to lift spirits—the live ones and the dead ones.

"Your friends are here, Brie." Mrs. Vo touches Brie's hands.

Brie opens her eyes. She lifts her legs off the couch and

raises herself to a sitting position without using her arms.

"How's your fin feel?" Willa asks.

"It hurts." Then she adds, "This is the worst."

"Sorry, Brie." I sit on the floor near the coffee table, grab a milk cake, and let the sweetness melt on my tongue. It's a thousand times better than any breakfast I could have eaten at home.

"At the meet last Saturday," Brie says, "I had a personal record in the two hundred 'fly."

"Because you're three-quarters dolphin." Willa sits down next to Brie on the couch.

Brie smiles just a little. "Then I swam the stupid two hundred IM, and I smacked my arm on the lane line during the backstroke. Totally tweaked my shoulder. I hate the backstroke."

Brie's voice cracks. Her eyes are watery. "My mom already found me a physical therapist. She's even paying him to come to our house, beginning today."

"That's good," I say. "You'll heal quickly with good therapy." That's what Hank always says, anyway.

But Brie doesn't answer, and now tears drip down her cheeks.

"Hey." Willa puts her arm around Brie's good shoulder. "You'll fix the fin. You'll hit another PR by the end of August."

Brie shakes her head. "No. You guys don't get it. I don't

care about personal records. I don't even want to swim anymore."

And now she sobs.

"Part of me"—Brie sniffs loudly—"was so happy when I hurt my shoulder." She sniffs again. "I thought I could quit. I could be done." More sniffing. "I could stop all the training, all the meets, all the"—she inhales deeply—"pressure."

I set my third milk cake back on the plate. I didn't know she hated swimming so much. She's so good. I thought you loved things you were good at, like I love computers and writing programs.

"Brie, I'm sorry," I say again. And I really am. "Have you told your parents you want to quit?"

"No." Brie wipes her eyes. "They wouldn't let me. They would spontaneously combust or something."

"But you can't keep doing something that makes you unhappy." I know this is true. It's exactly why I avoid Hank and Coral's activities every moment I can. It's why I find my own things to do. It's why I want the prize money from the hunt so badly—to make *me* happy for a change.

"My mom says I was born to swim."

That's kind of ridiculous, I think. Are people really born to do one thing? And if so, does that one thing have to be what your *parents* say it will be?

I'm not going to let that happen to me, and I don't think Brie should either.

Willa sits there silently, keeping her arm around Brie. What could she say, though? Her parents don't force her to do anything she doesn't want. They support her fully in whatever she does, like perfect parents should.

Willa finally speaks. "Well, more time for dancing with me!" She stands up. "I know. We'll do that Irish dancing where you keep your arms straight and don't use them." Willa makes two fists, locks her elbows, and glues them to her sides. Then she starts bouncing up and down, kicking her heels out side to side.

Willa has a dance for every occasion.

"And more time for the food cart hunt too," I add. "I found the fourth clue yesterday."

But Brie doesn't seem very happy about my news. "Just six more to find," I remind her.

"Mac." Brie rubs her shoulder. "I'm out of the hunt."

"What?"

"I'm going to be doing therapy every day, and when I'm not doing that, my parents will watch over me like I'm their inmate. So, yeah, I'm out."

I don't know what to say. I've been counting on Brie. No one calms me down and reminds me to relax and let things go like she can, especially when it comes to Hank and Coral.

I don't like that she's out, but I think I understand. She doesn't really have a choice.

At least I still have Willa.

Chapter Twenty

Willa's Crisis

"Let's hear about the clue you found yesterday," Willa says. "Maybe Brie can help us get started."

I pull out the napkin from my hunt folder and read aloud. "'Green, gold, and purple spices might get your arm strong. Shrimpy legs don't let you dance, but you can sing a song.'"

"I don't like that part about not dancing," Willa says.

"It's just a clue. It's not a command," I say.

Willa and I each grab another milk cake and eat slowly.

"You definitely need to order shrimp," Brie says.

"Right." I pull out my list of carts and food types and set it on the table, so we can all see it. "There's a lot we can rule out. It won't be a coffee cart or a bakery cart."

"And probably not breakfast or burgers either," Brie says.

Willa points to the list. "What about Brazilian? Do they eat shrimp in Brazil?"

I shrug. "We could look that up. Brie, can we use your laptop?"

She goes down the hallway and into another room and returns with her computer. Willa and I sit on each side of her on the couch as she logs in, then searches for popular Brazilian foods.

I read over her shoulder. "It looks like they mostly eat meats and fresh fruit, but here's something about dried shrimp, so I guess we can't rule it out. Go to the Portland Food Cart Association page," I tell Brie.

She types it into the search bar and the site pops up. We all stare at the screen.

"It could be any of the Thai, Chinese, Vietnamese, Cajun, Indian, or Indonesian carts," Brie says.

"We're not narrowing it down much," Willa says. "I don't have enough money or a big enough stomach to buy food at all those carts."

"And we don't have enough time." I feel the immense weight of the remaining five days.

"What about those spices the clue mentions?" Willa asks. "Must be special shrimp spices."

"Yeah," I say. "Green spices could be almost anything— oregano, basil, sage, cilantro. Maybe gold spices are like curry?"

"And what are purple spices?" Brie asks.

"No idea," I say.

Willa's phone beeps, and she looks away from the computer to read a text.

Brie switches back to the tab listing all the carts and begins counting. "Mac, this is hundreds of carts. Some of them are as far away as Gresham and some are way out on the west side."

"I know. Click on the news tab."

Brie does, and I scan the list. It's looks the same as last time—just short sentences about carts and changes and openings. Nothing about the hunt.

Willa's phone beeps again. She reads the text but doesn't respond. She sits still, gripping her phone.

"We should make a decision about where to go, Willa." I'm not giving up. I need this prize money. "I like the idea of visiting some of these Indian food carts and reading some menus. There's one on Foster Road we can start with. It wouldn't take us very long to get there."

Willa keeps staring at her phone.

I keep thinking aloud. "I'm wondering if there's some trick to this shrimp clue. Something like the tagine clue. Those spice colors seem important, but what do—"

Willa stands up and puts her phone into her front pocket. "I have to go."

I throw up my arms. "What do you mean you have to

go? We're trying to figure out this clue, Willa."

"Yeah, well, I'm out too," Willa says. "I'm off the team."

"No, you're not." I lightly slap her wrist.

Willa sits back down on the edge of the couch. Her face is unreadable to me. I've never seen her look so . . . blank. "Those texts I just got were from my mom, and the last one was from my dad, saying it's true."

"Oh, Willa." Brie leans forward and takes Willa's hand.

"Oh, Willa, what? What's going on?" I look at my friends, first Willa, then Brie, then back to Willa. My eyes flick like Ping-Pong balls.

"My dad's moving out." Willa stares at me. "To live with his girlfriend. And Mom just filed for divorce. So, yeah, I have to go."

Wait.

What?

Willa gets up and walks across the living room to the front door. There's none of the Willa dance or lightness in her entire being. It's like she's slogging through a thick, muddy river. "Good luck, Mac."

My mouth hangs open, as if I'm slowly sinking in her muddy river.

Willa's parents are getting divorced? Her father has a girlfriend? How could he?

I always thought her parents . . .

"Brie? Did you know?"

She nods.

This explains all the weirdness from Willa. Her spending time with just her dad and Becca. Her mom's tears that I witnessed the other morning.

"Willa told me they were arguing a lot. She said it was getting intense at home. I think she knew this was coming."

I've never thought it was intense at Willa's house. It's always been a perfect comfort home, from the first time I ever stepped into it. There's reclining sofas and chairs, gaming systems, a refrigerator with sugary sodas. Her mom drives a Chrysler minivan. Her dad wears a tie to his downtown office job. Her parents are normal professional adults, like the adult I once thought Coho was.

Willa has no chickens, no Earth festivals, no living room futon island.

No weirdness.

"Why didn't she say anything to me?" I ask Brie.

But I also wonder why I didn't piece it all together. There were so many clues, like all the texting, and how she was doing stuff with her dad, and how her parents were so quiet at the end-of-the-year picnic, not talking, turned away from each other, and Willa sitting between them, silent and still. That wasn't normal.

I stare at Brie's laptop. The food cart website fades away

and a picture of a much younger Brie winning a swimming trophy half her size appears on the screen.

"Brie?" Her mother steps into the living room. "You have therapy in ten minutes."

Brie nods at her mom, then grabs my hand and squeezes it. "Mac, I'm sorry we can't help you on the hunt right now."

"I'm sorry too," I say. "I don't mean about the hunt—I mean about Willa and her parents, and you and your shoulder. I'm sorry."

"I know." Brie squeezes my hand again.

I walk home, taking a long route, thinking about the past few days and how I'm such a rotten friend. How could I not have known about all the pressure Brie's parents put on her to succeed in swimming, and how much she hates it?

A silver minivan rolls by, and I think of Willa's mom and the perfect smell of her van. But clearly, nothing's perfect in that car or in that house. How could I be such an idiot? Everything's going to be different for her now. She's probably not dancing.

What if she never dances again?

It's about noon when I get home. Coral's near the coop garage with a group of adults, including Coho. They all have their bicycles. The goats are chomping on the hay Coho spread for them in the yard. The White Leghorns are pecking the ground around them.

I recognize a few of the people. They're part of Coral's bicycling club.

"MacKenna." Coral moves toward me and pulls me in for a hug. "I'm doing some fittings and adjustments for our big bike ride on Saturday evening. We've all got to be ready." She winks.

I note her wink, but I don't ask any questions. I know with Coral that it's usually best to smile and move on.

"MacKenna's doing food cart research this summer," she announces to her group. "Finding the locally sustainable carts."

There's a general hum of oohs and aahs from the bicycling club.

One guy says, "I heard a bunch of carts are going to be at Cathedral Park for the ride on Saturday. We can get some grub before we streak off down the roads."

Everyone laughs except me. Four or five hours earlier, that comment may have interested me. It may have been useful and worth checking out for the hunt, but not anymore.

Because my research is finished. I won't be decoding hunt clues anymore. I won't be going to coding camp either.

I pretty much figured that out on my walk home. It was an easy code to write.

Joey Marino can take the whole prize money and go open a library for the homeless, or whatever his next great community project will be. I'll be stuck here with Hank and Coral, defending Coral's garden from the yoga goats, feeding an evil chicken, sitting in drum circles . . . the life of Hippie Chick Goat Girl.

The food cart hunt is over. I'm off the team too.

Chapter Twenty-One

A Decision

After dinner, I retreat to my futon island. Hank, Coral, and Coho stay in the kitchen. I hear their voices. They're discussing how to get Ziggy, Marley, and Emmylou to be more active during their goat yoga sessions. Hank says something about making a new drum. Coral says something about a naked bike ride, but I don't hear any details, and I'm certainly not going to ask. I feel too empty to even worry about it right now.

I stare at my poster, whispering the words aloud: "'Girls Are Supercoders.'"

Since there won't be any coding for me this summer, I'll have to wait and see what Mrs. Naberhaus teaches us next year. By the time I'm in high school, I'll be way behind everyone else. I'll always be playing catch-up because I'll always be lagging behind, living with Hank and Coral.

I thought this hunt was my answer, but it was only a

stupid dream. Did I really believe going to a computer camp behind Hank and Coral's back was possible? And, even crazier, did I really believe I could wander all over town, searching for clues from food carts to win money to pay for the camp? What were my odds? Microscopically slim, that's what they were.

And now there aren't any odds to calculate because I'm out of the hunt.

I pull the folder with the clues and notes out of my bag. One last time, I look at the four clues I have. The first one that I had to write on a bookmark because Joey picked up the original. The second clue on the cup sleeve from the double-decker bus. The third clue from the napkin with the tagine, and the fourth one on the napkin around the Sunshine Tropics smoothie. I lay them out on my blanket and read them all one more time. Then I place them back in the folder and tuck the whole thing under my futon.

I find my little flipper and send texts to Willa and Brie to check in with them.

Willa doesn't answer.

Brie responds, telling me she's okay and that Willa hasn't answered her texts either.

Around nine p.m., I get another text from Brie: You should keep doing the hunt.

But I don't respond, because I'm not going to continue. Besides, I only have $4.15 in my life savings now. There's no way I could keep hunting on my own. I toss my flipper on the bed and realize I need to figure out how to pay back Coho.

I'll talk with Mr. Z about dog walking tomorrow.

And maybe I could offer to babysit Willa's little sister, Becca, so Willa can do what she needs to do with her mom or her dad. I won't charge them, though. I'll do that for free. I owe Willa that much.

And I'll keep Brie company every day when she does her shoulder therapy.

That's going to be my summer now.

About ten o'clock, I finally get a text from Willa: Don't give up on the hunt.

I tap out a response: You okay?

Willa: Managing.

I realize that's probably what she's been doing for months. Managing.

Willa texts me again: Did you read me? Don't give up on the hunt.

Me: The hunt's done.

Willa: Doesn't have to be.

I don't text back, and my phone buzzes again. It's Willa once more: Keep hunting!

I stare at my phone for a few long moments before tapping: Willa, I'm really sorry.

Then I add one final text: For everything.

I lie there on my island, thinking of Willa and Brie. Their texts keep scrolling in my head.

Did you read me? Don't give up on the hunt.

Keep hunting.

But there's no point in continuing.

There's only four days left.

Certainly, there are others who have more than four clues. Joey Marino probably does. There may be someone who already has all ten! Could be that Shaggy and Scarface duo. There's just no chance for me.

But I reach under my futon, and I slide out the folder, pulling out the clue from the smoothie cart.

"'Green, gold, and purple,'" I say out loud.

I know those colors are a major hint.

Keep hunting.

"'Shrimpy legs don't let you dance, but you can sing a song.'" I stare at the fourth clue.

What if . . .

I really need to stop thinking about this hunt and these clues, but what if . . . what if I had someone else to help me?

What if I just asked . . .

What am I thinking?

No way.

My mind ticks back and forth. Ask! Stop! Ask! Stop!

I clasp my head, trying to squeeze away the relentless pendulum in my brain.

I stare at my poster again. *Girls Are Supercoders.*

I can't quit.

I can't.

I've never quit when I've had challenging computer programs. I've always gone over every step, troubleshooting the whole way.

So I *will* keep hunting. And I'll ask Joey Marino to join my team.

But the problem is, I'll have to find him. I don't know where he lives. I don't know his number, and I doubt Willa or Brie would have it either.

How do you find someone who's a phantom?

Chapter Twenty-Two

Patsy's Diner

I gather the chicken eggs in the morning and return to the kitchen to find Coho standing there, holding open his wallet. I gulp and cling to the basket handle. He's counting his money!

"Hey, Mac!" He pulls out a bill and shoves it in his pocket.

Does he know?

I blink at him. He said eye blinking was calming.

His eyebrows are neutral. That's good.

He's smiling. That's good.

I blink again.

"How's the research going?" Coho asks.

His voice doesn't sound suspicious at all. Maybe he doesn't know. I relax my grip on the basket.

There's so much I want to ask Coho, like why in the world would he throw away his career? Why is he here bringing us goats and an ill-behaved chicken? I want to tell him how betrayed I feel, but Hank stumbles into the kitchen, rubbing his eyes, and my moment is lost.

It's just as well because I need to find Joey Marino today, and I thought of a way to locate him. Since I don't have his apparitional skills, I must use the skills I do have. Searching the internet. I have one clue. It's the name tag I saw on the woman who spoke with Joey in the hallway on our last day of school. Her tag said *Patsy's Diner.*

The Belmont Library doesn't open until ten, so I text Brie, hoping she's up and will see my message and do some internet searching for me: What's the address of Patsy's Diner?

Three minutes pass, and Brie responds: 372 SE Alder. Why?

It's tedious texting on my flipper phone. I want to tell Brie that I'm still hunting, that I'm going to ask Joey Marino to help, that I think I know where his mom works. I want to ask how her shoulder feels and if she's heard from Willa this morning, but I stick with the questions I need answered right now.

Me: What bus do I take?

Two more minutes pass, then: 15. Get off at Morrison and Grand. WHY?

Me: Thanks!

In my mind, I'm sending her smiley and heart emojis. I will tell her later.

***

At nine fifteen, I step off the bus and walk two blocks to Patsy's Diner. There's a glass door that drags heavily across the floor as I push it open. The diner is small, maybe twenty tables, and there's customers at each one. Most are old and are sipping their coffee and eating their scrambled eggs and pancakes. Two women in brown dresses are scurrying around with pitchers of water and plates of food in their hands. One woman sees me and slides her notepad into her apron pocket. She moves toward me, still holding the pitcher. "You all alone?"

I recognize her tight bun and the gray hair streaks. It's the woman who spoke with Joey at school.

"Yes, but I'm not here to eat, I just have a question."

"You need to speak to Clyde?" she asks.

I shake my head. "No, to you, actually."

"Me? Do I know you?"

I look at her name tag. Under *Patsy's Diner* it says *Aggie*.

"I'm . . . um . . . just wondering if you're Joey's mom. Joey Marino, from Winterhill School?"

She puts the pitcher down on a nearby table. The man sitting there grumbles, but Aggie ignores him. "You're a friend of Joey's?"

Friend?

No, not really.

Only an acquaintance. But I say, "Yes, and I wanted to

140

ask him something about his school projects, but I don't have his number." It was the line I'd rehearsed on the bus ride here.

Aggie's eyes widen. "What's your name?"

"Mac."

"Joey doesn't talk much about his friends at school." She wipes her hands on her apron.

Joey doesn't talk much at all, I want to say.

Grumbling Man at the table mutters again about the water pitcher, and Aggie grabs it, fills his glass, and then steps away from the table, motioning for me to follow.

"Aggie! It's not your break time." It's a barking voice from the back of the diner, probably the kitchen, but I don't see a face.

"This is my son's friend, Clyde. Give me a few," she hollers back.

"You get one!" Clyde-from-the-back shouts.

"Would you be able to give me his number?" I ask, and I can't help but wonder if normal parents do this sort of thing. Do they give out their child's phone number to a stranger? I don't think I look intimidating or scary. I smile at her, and she looks like she wants to hug me.

"Aggie!"

She makes a fist, and I want to storm back there and tell Clyde about all the negative energies that he's releasing each time he yells. That's what Coral would do.

Aggie pulls out her order notepad and scribbles down a number. She tears off the paper and puts it in my palm. "Please call him," she says. "He needs a friend."

And so does she, I think.

"Aggie!"

"I'm working, Clyde!"

I watch her for a moment as she scurries to another table, grabs a pot of coffee, and fills mugs at several tables. In my head I'm pseudocoding her steps into a computer game: *Turn 180 degrees. Move 200 steps. Open kitchen door. Remove apron. Throw apron at Clyde. Shout "I quit!"*

Joey's mom doesn't deserve this treatment.

No one does.

But I leave the diner and pull out my flipper phone, tapping a text to the number on the slip of paper: It's Mac. Can we meet somewhere?

One minute later, my phone buzzes: Brooklyn Park. 30 minutes.

Chapter Twenty-Three

A Proposal

Joey Marino sits on a swing in the Brooklyn Park playground when I arrive. He's twisting in the seat, side to side, the toes of his combat boots dragging in the bark chips, forming a figure eight below him.

The park is mostly empty this time of day. Down on the field, a man tosses a tennis ball to his black Lab. A woman leans against the chain-link fence, a blanket wrapped around her shoulders even though it's probably seventy degrees out.

Joey says nothing as I walk toward him and sit on the swing next to him. "Hi," I begin.

He nods but still doesn't say anything.

"You're probably wondering why I texted you."

"How'd you get my number?"

"Your mom."

He freezes for a moment.

"I saw your mom the last day of school, and she was

wearing a Patsy's Diner name tag, so I found out where that was and went to see her."

"Oh" is all he says.

We twist silently back and forth on our swings while I consider how to begin the conversation. I inhale deeply. "So, I have a proposal."

Joey looks up, a rare half grin on his pale face. "We're too young to get married, Mac."

"What?" I frown at him. "That's not what I'm talking about. I'm proposing . . ." His response has me rattled. I inhale again. "I was thinking that we could team up on the food cart hunt. I know you're doing it too."

He shoves his boot soles into the bark chips and stops twisting the swing. "What happened to Willa and Brie?"

"They're a little busy right now."

He starts to rock back and forth on the swing slowly, his toes staying on the ground. "Why are you doing the hunt?"

"Why are *you* doing it?"

"I asked you first."

I push off and begin swinging, pumping my legs. "I need money."

"For what?" Joey swings too.

"A camp, and maybe some other things." This is our longest conversation ever, by far. "It's the summer coding camp at our school. I want to go."

"You want to write computer programs all summer?"

"Actually, I do."

Joey's eyes are like drills, boring holes through me.

"Look, you don't know what it's like for me in the summer. All year long, actually. Living with my parents is nothing you could ever imagine."

"How's that?"

"Well, they . . ." I don't know where to start. I drag my shoes into the bark chips and stop swinging. I hold out my hand to show Joey my stab wounds. "These are from a stupid chicken that I have to feed and collect eggs from every morning."

Joey peers at the back of my hand. "Vicious."

He's mocking me like all the other kids at school.

"It's horrible at home, okay? You've seen my parents at school, right? My mom with her plastic-filled dreadlocks? My dad with his drum?"

Joey doesn't answer.

"Guess what they got two days ago? Goats. Goats for yoga."

"Can you do that? Have goats at your house, I mean?" Joey's laughing. It's a sound I've never heard.

"No!" And I can't help it, I laugh too.

"See? That's how weird they are," I continue. "You saw my mom the other day at the Joan of Arc statue. Do you remember?"

"The naked bikers?"

"She was wearing kale," I add.

"It was more than some of the others." He laughs again. "So, you're hunting for food cart clues, hoping to win money so that you can go to camp all day and learn how to code little programs to make games that will help you avoid your parents riding their bikes naked and doing goat yoga."

"No!" I kick at the bark chips. "That's not—"

I think I like Joey Marino better when he's silent and mysterious. His words make me feel ridiculous, and selfish, and pea brained. I hate that I feel tears forming.

"I happen to like computers and writing programs. I'm good at it, and I want to get better, but maybe you don't get that." I rise off the swing, flick the seat away from me, and start walking away. "Forget it, Joey. Forget the whole proposal."

"Mac, come back." Joey gets off his swing too. "Hey, I'm sorry."

I turn around and look at him, his not-so-clear skin shiny and oily, his gray shirt wrinkled and drab. I wipe my eyes and move back to the swing and sit. Joey does the same.

"Hank and Coral don't get me," I say. "They never have. I feel like I was adopted or switched at birth, or like they just found me in their garden one day and plucked me off a vine." I swing slowly. "Years ago, I begged them for a tablet, but they looked at me stunned, like I'd asked for a weapon or something. They said staring at a tablet would expose my brain to all the vices of the world. Hank and Coral never listen to my reasons. I don't think they ever will."

Joey doesn't interrupt me. I have no idea why I'm suddenly sharing this stuff with him, but now that I've started, I can't seem to stop. "Living with Hank and Coral is like growing up in the 1920s except . . . on a stupid urban farm with less cool clothes. They don't understand that things are different now. We can go to stores for our vegetables, and we can even buy organic there. We don't have to spend a full day making soap and candles. They don't see the beauty in technology the way I do. They don't . . ." I shake my head.

Joey nods at me, like he wants me to keep going, like he's really listening.

"I just think having money to go to this camp will give me some breathing room and some time to do what I want. Not what they want. I'm too young to get a job, so when I found out about the hunt, it seemed perfect, and fun too." I pause. "I really, *really* want this prize money. I don't know what else to say about it."

Joey thrusts out his boots and begins pumping the swing. I'm waiting for him to respond, but he just silently rises higher and higher with each leg pump. I do the same. Our swings aren't in sync. He's back when I'm forward. I'm forward when he's back.

"Hey." I speak loudly. "Your turn. Why are you doing the hunt?"

"I need money too," he says.

"Why?"

But Joey doesn't answer. He just keeps swinging. Back and forth. Back and forth.

Finally, he says, "For my mom."

My legs stop pumping.

Aggie.

Joey's mom, with the nonstop job at Patsy's Diner and a boss who needs an attitude adjustment. Joey's mom, who loves her son. That was easy to see.

But I didn't expect that answer. I figured he wanted money for his next great community project. Maybe that library for the homeless.

"Oh." That's all I say. My swinging slows.

Joey stops pumping his legs too. "She's sick."

Sick? She didn't look sick to me. She just looked tired, and sad, and maybe a little angry.

"Is it serious?"

Joey jams his combat boots into the bark chips and pops out of the seat of his swing. He starts walking away from me. I jump off my swing and follow him, jogging to keep up.

"I have two moms," he finally says.

"What?" I touch his shoulder, forcing him to stop and turn around.

"Two moms. Okay?" He faces me, eyebrows lifted.

"Okay. I just . . . I didn't know that. You never mentioned it."

"No one's ever asked."

Oh.

He's right. I've never asked him . . . anything, until today. I don't think Willa or Brie or anyone else has either. He's always been such a . . . mystery.

"My ma, the one you met, is fine other than working so much. It's my other mom who I need to get money for."

I feel a sense of relief for Aggie, the mom I met, but I ask, "Does your other mom live in Portland?"

"Yeah, but she doesn't live with us."

We slowly make our way toward the bleachers near the baseball diamond.

"I don't think I've seen your other mom," I say, which is such a dumb comment. I've only seen Aggie twice.

Joey stops. "Actually, you have. You just didn't know who she was."

Chapter Twenty-Four

Joey's Connections

"What do you mean? When did I see her?" I ask.

We climb onto the small set of metal bleachers behind the baseball backstop and sit on the middle bench.

"I think you've seen her a few times, but that doesn't really matter right now. The only thing that matters is that I win this prize money, so I can help her."

I scroll through my memories, trying to think of when I may have seen Joey's other mom, and I can't think of any time. At school, Joey's always by himself. I wonder what's wrong with his mom. How sick is she? I should ask because apparently, I don't do that enough.

I start to form a question when Joey blurts out, "Right now, you and I should focus on this hunt, not our parents."

He's right. Our hunting minutes are precious and dwindling. Saturday is just three days away. We have clues to locate. I'll ask about Joey's mom another time.

"So, that means we're officially a team?"

"Sure." Joey sticks out his hand. "I suppose we should shake on it. Prize money will be split?"

"Deal." I grasp his hand.

Splitting the money in half rather than thirds gives me an instant jolt of energy.

One thousand dollars each!

"How many clues do you have?" I ask.

Joey yanks off his stuffed backpack and pulls out what looks like a wad of trash. He lays out napkins and papers on the bleacher bench in front of us.

"Seven," he says.

"Seven!" I pick them up one at a time. "How did you solve so many?"

"It's not about solving," he says. "It's about connections."

"What are you talking about?"

"I know people," he says. "How many do you have?"

I pull out the four clues from my hunt folder and hand them to Joey.

He reads them over. "I don't have this one." He holds up the *sunshine tropics* clue that led me to Smoothie Guy.

"You were totally following me the other day to get another clue."

Joey grins. "You were my connection, Mac. Thanks."

I pick up a couple of his clues that I don't have. "'Take a shot in the dark if you dare. Be large and be whole since you care,'" I read. "Where was this cart?"

Joey shrugs. "No idea."

"Then how'd you get it?"

He flicks my forehead with his fingers. "You're not using your logical brain. I keep telling you. I have connections. This clue was given to me." He reaches down and picks up three more. "So were these." He waves them in my face. "You left this clue on the table, remember?"

He's holding up my first clue, the one I got from Lorenzo, which led to the fish and chips on the double-decker bus. "This is the only clue I've actually solved."

I'm a little confused, and a lot amazed.

"Snitch gave me this one about creamy, spicy, and sweet. He hangs out between Division and Clinton Street. He's a Gulf War vet and has PTSD, but he counsels other vets at the Eastbank Shelter when he's having a good day," Joey explains.

"A homeless guy gave you this clue?"

He picks up a crinkled paper next and reads it aloud. "One meat, one fruit. Can you find the mate? It just might come from a small red state." He glances at me. "This clue came from Yolanda. She stays at a camp near the river. Told me she found it picking through trash one day and thought it was a message from the Holy Ghost."

Another homeless person?

Right then, all of Joey's actions over the past few days

begin to make sense. He's constantly talking to homeless people and giving them stuff. There's the woman he handed his travel mug to. There's the man he gave a granola bar to, the one with the barking dog. There's the woman downtown he gave the book to, who then grabbed him, and I scared her off.

This is how Joey gets the clues.

Unbelievable.

My face must display all my shock because he says, "If you want to know what's going on in the city, you ask people who are on the streets all day and night. Some of them know more than the cops. More than any of us."

Unbelievable.

Joey Marino looks like he's twelve, but he speaks like he's eighty.

He rearranges all the clues on the bleacher bench, his and mine. "Together we have eight clues, Mac."

Eight clues!

I feel a gust of fresh air, like good fortune. With eight clues between us and all of Joey Marino's connections, finding two more clues in four days might be possible. Winning this hunt could really happen.

I lean over and scan all the clues, flipping over the ones that have been solved, which is only three. That leaves us with five unsolved clues. "The problem is," I say with a sigh, "that one or more of these clues"—I point to the five unsolved—"will just lead us to a clue that we already have."

But I won't let that set me back. We have eight clues! Double what I had just twenty minutes ago.

I pick up a clue on waxy paper.

Jack might know how to divide the white.
So squeeze the citrus and take a bite.

"Joey! I know where this clue leads to."

Chapter Twenty-Five

Pepper or Monterey

Joey and I catch the 4 bus and head east on Division Street, back to the cart pod I'd visited just a few days earlier. As soon as I sit down, I send texts to Willa and Brie to let them know I'm still hunting and teaming with Joey. Then I begin telling Joey about Shaggy and Scarface, and how I spied them reading the menu at the grilled cheese cart.

"I overheard them say the word *jack*, but then I wasn't able to see what they actually ordered." I don't mention that it was him and a barking dog that distracted me. "I'm pretty sure we should order the sandwich with jack cheese on white bread. I think the word *divide* is a reference to Division Street, and the 'squeeze the citrus' is the drink. We probably need to order orange juice, or maybe lemonade."

It's simple, like a four-step computer program. *Go to Division Street pod. Order one grilled cheese. Order one citrus drink. Receive the next clue.*

Girls are supercoders!

Joey appears unmoved by my brilliant display of decoding skills. He looks out the bus window, more focused on the people outside the bus than on me.

His distracted silence doesn't make me feel like we're much of a team. I seem to be doing all the thinking and planning.

When the bus coasts to a stop at 28th and Division, Joey and I hop off and cross 28th to the food cart pod. It's about an hour before the lunch eaters will arrive, so it's not overly crowded like on my first visit. No one's in line at Greg's Grilled Cheese, so I stand in front of the orange trailer and read the menu board.

"There're three problems," I say. "Number one: Do we order pepper or Monterey Jack? Number two: Lemonade or orange juice? They have both. Number three: I only have four dollars and fifteen cents."

I remember all the coins Joey pulled out of his backpack the other day on the way to the zoo. He's going to have to cover us for most of this meal and potential clue.

Now I'll owe Coho and Joey.

But the winning cash I'll reel in on Saturday will cover my debts. I'm feeling positive now. I almost feel like dancing, like Willa would do.

"Stay here." Joey points to the pavement, like I'm

suddenly his dog in training. Not a very team-like thing to do.

"Wait. What are you doing?"

Joey walks up to the order window and talks to the woman inside the grilled cheese trailer. He's leaning in and whispering, so I can't hear a word that's said.

He doesn't really think this woman will just hand over the clue without ordering, does he? He clearly doesn't understand this hunt. These carts aren't involved for fun. They're in it because it will make them some money.

After several minutes of discussion, Joey returns empty-handed.

"What was that about?" I ask.

Joey doesn't answer. He swings his backpack off his shoulders, unzips it, and pulls out a baseball cap. Smoothing his long bangs to the side, he sticks the cap on his head and says, "Ready?"

"Ready for what?"

"To work."

"What?"

But Joey doesn't answer me. He moves toward the grilled cheese cart and vanishes behind it. I jog to catch up to him. He stands by three large bins. "The woman has lots for us to do. We'll earn our food and the next clue. We'll start here."

Work for food. Work for the clue. This must be how he

got the clue at the double-decker bus.

My shoulders slump. This is not the most efficient means of getting the clue, but without money, I don't have much choice.

We begin by sorting garbage, recycling, and compost. We open the bins, and Joey immediately pulls out plastic water bottles and cans from the garbage bin and tosses them into the recycling bin.

"I'm going to go ask for gloves." I can't believe I'm diving in dumpsters.

When I come back with too-big plastic gloves, Joey gives me a new order. "Connect that red hose with the nozzle to the spigot over there. She told me all the carts can use that for cleanup."

I prefer the quiet, ghostlike Joey to this bossy version, but I do what he says and pull the end of the hose to the bins where he takes the nozzle from me and proceeds to rinse out cardboard containers that can be recycled. Joey hands me a plastic fork. "Use this to scrape the large chunks of food into the compost bin. Put napkins in there too."

Disgusting, I think to myself, but I also think of Hank and Coral, two people who'd be proud to see me sorting trash, especially with someone as community minded as Joey Marino. I'm practically shrinking my carbon footprint by a whole shoe size right now.

Soon the woman appears and sets down a bucket with soapy water. "This is to wash the exterior of the trailer," she says. "Make sure you rinse periodically so that the soap doesn't leave streaks and be sure not to get water inside."

Joey washes a section near the back with soapy water and a rag. I spray it down when he's done, watching the soap suds stream away. I think about how if Willa and Brie were here instead of Joey Marino, the clue would already be in my hands because they would help me pay.

Then again, I wouldn't have Joey's clues, which means I wouldn't have a shot at winning the money.

After completing the exterior wash, we move inside the cart. The woman hands us some sort of salt paste and a cloth and tells us to wipe down her griddle. I start on the right side and Joey on the left side. We work over every inch of the cast iron. It's strangely satisfying to wipe away the stuck bits of cheese and bread, kind of like pushing away Hank and Coral's clutter surrounding my futon island. The surface slowly begins to shine.

If Coral had a griddle like this, I'd clean it every day if she'd fry me some bacon with our eggs . . . and the occasional burger.

"Just one more thing," the woman says. She points to the knives and two blocks of cheese. "Wash your hands well, then slice some thick chunks for me."

My stomach rages. I hope we can eat soon.

After what feels like a forty-hour workweek, we finish the slicing.

"Aren't you two darlings," Grilled Cheese Woman says. "What can I make for you? I bet you're hungry."

I whisper instructions to Joey and he places our order. "She'll have pepper jack on white with orange juice, and I'll have Monterey Jack on white with lemonade."

The woman nods at us and tells us to go outside and wait at the tables. "I'll bring your food when it's ready."

Joey pulls off his hat and shoves it in his backpack as soon as we sit down. His hair is damp and sticks to his forehead.

He points at my palm. "I think you have a blister."

I inspect quickly. He's right. There are small blisters on both my hands.

Grilled Cheese Woman walks toward us and sets down our sandwiches, drinks, and napkins. "Here's the receipt for your services." She tucks the slip of paper under Joey's foil-wrapped sandwich and gives him a wink.

I grab the receipt before Joey can and read the words printed on the back:

Take a shot in the dark if you dare.
Be large and be whole since you care.

I slam my fist down on the table. "We just worked our butts off for a clue that we already have. What a waste of time."

Joey picks up the paper, reads it, then slides it into his backpack. "The world's a cleaner place now because of us, Mac. At least her cart is."

I stare at all his grayness. There's dismay mixed into his words.

Because a cleaner world and a clean grilled-cheese cart doesn't get me closer to my computer camp, or him closer to helping his mom.

Chapter Twenty-Six

A Visit with Brie

Joey and I finish our sandwiches. Good food always puts me in a better mood. "Let's plan our next move."

"Can't," Joey says. "Ma's working a double shift at the diner today. I have to get back to our apartment, make her some dinner, and do a few other things."

"But . . ." I try to hold in my disappointment, but it's clearly oozing from my face.

"We'll find another clue tomorrow, Mac." He stands up. "We can start early. I'll come by your house about eight."

"No!"

That's a bad idea. Coral will suck him in and gush about his cafeteria composting and free-food-table projects. Hank will want every detail about the new water systems Joey helped the school get. Within an hour, they'll be telling him he can come by anytime, or even move in.

"Let's meet somewhere. Maybe Sunnyville School? It's close to the main bus lines."

"I'll text you." Joey waves and tosses his backpack over his shoulder.

I sit at the table and watch him walk away, feeling strangely empty, even with a nourished stomach. I remind myself that we have eight clues.

Two more clues, and I'll have one thousand dollars. I'll be learning new coding languages. Creating apps and games.

I check my phone for texts. Willa hasn't responded, but Brie has: Come by. Doing physical therapy.

I hop on the bus for ten blocks, then walk to Brie's house. Mrs. Vo lets me in, and I see Brie lying over a highly inflated yoga ball, belly down. Her arms are out to her sides like butterfly wings.

"Shoulder exercise?" I ask.

"Yes, and it hurts." Brie's voice strains. She holds her arms out for about five more seconds and then rolls off the ball and kicks it hard against the wall.

Mrs. Vo rushes back in. "Brie? Are you okay?"

"I'm fine, Mom. I'm going to take a break."

"You can exercise with your friend here." Mrs. Vo points a finger at the yoga ball.

Brie kicks it again as her mom leaves the room. "The physical therapist was here for two hours this morning teaching me exercises. Mom took notes the entire time. I really want to be done." She whispers the last sentence.

"You don't have to do everything your parents want." I tell myself this a lot.

"You don't understand. My parents are so . . ." Brie turns her head away from me and breathes out. "I don't want to talk about them or my shoulder. I'm so glad you're still doing the hunt. How's it going?"

I sit down next to her on the carpet and tell her about my day with Joey, all the clues he has, how he and I are teaming up to find the final two clues, how he talked the grilled cheese lady into letting us work for the next clue, but then how it was all for nothing. The only thing I don't mention is Joey's other mom, and how she's sick.

"I'm glad you have someone to help, but Joey Marino? I don't think I've ever talked to him." Brie speaks softly.

I get how she feels. I had the same thought yesterday, how none of us has ever tried to talk to Joey. I'm not proud of that either.

I quickly change the subject. "Have you heard from Willa? She hasn't answered my text."

"Yes. She said her dad's packing a bunch of his stuff up at the house. She's hanging out with her mom and Becca at their aunt's place until her dad's done and out completely."

A stupid stab of jealousy hits me in the chest. Jealousy

that Brie knows this info and I don't. That Willa told her all this but not me.

"She says her mom might sell the house," Brie adds.

"What?"

The Moores' home? That beautiful, four-bedroom, two-bath home with a porch and a driveway? It's going to be sold?

"Where will they move?"

"An apartment in Northeast."

"But that's so far away. Can she still go to Winterhill?"

Brie rubs her bum shoulder and rolls it in circles. "I don't think she's worried about that right now."

That's probably true.

"Mac," Brie says, "Willa and I can't help with the hunt, but you know we're both cheering for you . . . and Joey."

"I know. Thanks."

Chapter Twenty-Seven

The Broody Chicken

On Thursday morning, Hank and Coral are once again already up, probably doing early morning goat yoga. But after I finish braiding my hair, I find Coral and Coho at the kitchen table with huge clumps of red rhododendrons in front of them. Coral has a needle and thread, and she's stitching the flowers together, poking her needle through the stems.

"What're you doing?"

As soon as I ask, I wish I hadn't. It's safest to keep far away from Coral and her crafts. She has a cyclone way of sweeping me into her recyclable decor projects. Two summers ago, she sucked me into collecting clear plastic CD cases. Then she made a chandelier out of them for our hallway. Last summer, she had me clean grease off extra bicycle chains and she super-glued them into baskets.

"Coho and I are making flowered leis for everyone to

wear at the bike ride on Saturday." She smiles at me. "I'd love your help, but Hank needs you more. He's out with the chickens."

The egg basket sits on the kitchen counter, and I peek inside. There're only three eggs.

I hear light tapping when I go outside. The garage door is open, and the goats are inside standing by Hank, who's sitting on the floor in the straw, his drum in his lap.

Rumpa-pum-pum.

Ziggy, Marley, and Emmylou all bounce toward me, circling me with their goat dance. I try to push them away, to keep their fur and smell off my clean clothes.

"Mac, good, you're here." Hank pauses his bongo beat. "I've already collected the eggs. We've got a problem to deal with."

"What problem?"

Emmylou pokes her head at my thigh.

"Look at Poppy."

The Rhode Island Red sits in a nesting box, staring forward with her permanent head tilt. She doesn't move or twitch.

"Does she seem broody to you?" Hank asks.

"Broody? She's not broody. She's just mean."

Hank ignores my comment. "I've been drumming for her this morning. I don't think it's helping."

Hank sets his drum down and gets up, moving to Poppy's

roost. He scoops her up, gently holding down her wings. He brings her tilted head to his lips and kisses it.

"She probably has a disease. And now you're going to get it."

Hank shakes his head. "No. I think it's the goats."

"What?"

"I think Poppy is jealous of them." Hank kisses his new evil hen one more time, and places her lovingly back on her straw pile.

"Maybe you should take the goats back." I want to suggest he give Poppy back too, but I keep that to myself.

"We're going to give the coop a thorough scouring," Hank states.

"But we did that last month." I don't have time for coop cleaning. The hunt clock is ticking—fast.

"I think cleaner living accommodations will help her feel that she's still adored. I also think we should build her a higher roost."

Hank's words make the blood in my whole body stop flowing. It's like I'm not even standing in this garage with him. Maybe I need to cluck. Maybe I need to bleat. Maybe I need to pound on his drum.

Doesn't he notice . . . me? I'm brooding too.

I turn away.

"Mac? You okay?"

"I have important things to do today." I still don't face

him, but it doesn't matter because he can't see me anyway. He can't see that the shorts and shoes I'm wearing are getting too small. He can't see all the things I'm good at, like math and programming. He can't see that I'm busy with my own things. He can't see that this chicken coop garage is not where I want to spend my time.

"We'll get this done today. I'm going to get a bale of straw and some fresh feed." Hank hitches his trailer to his bike.

"Hank, I—"

He hands me a push broom. "You can begin sweeping out the old straw. Your food cart research can wait, Mac."

He squeezes my shoulders in a one-armed hug. "Our chickens need you now."

Hank peddles down the driveway, and I'm stuck standing with a broom in a straw-filled garage, with four chickens and three prancing goats. "They're *not* my chickens!"

But Hank is already at the end of the block. I fling the broom onto the floor, nearly hitting Ziggy on her rump.

"And they don't need me!" I add. "Poppy doesn't even *like* me! I'm probably the reason she's broody!"

Ziggy and Marley seem to be the only creatures affected by my yelling. They dart out of the garage. But Emmylou stays, poking me with her nose over and over.

I grab the feeder container and take it out to the compost bin, tossing away the small amount of remaining feed.

Just as the last kernel falls out, I feel a sharp needle stab in my ankle. "Ouch!"

Poppy has followed me.

And now she's attacking me. She jabs her beak into my ankle again.

"Go away!" I kick at her. "I'm going to clean your coop, so back off." But it's impossible to reason with this tick-brained animal. She lifts her wings and shakes them, but she doesn't move. She leans forward to skewer me again. I hop backward, lifting my stabbed ankle away from her, and then . . .

WHAM!

I'm flat on my back on the lawn and a foot is on my chest.

No.

Make that a hoof.

Now two hooves.

Marley or maybe Ziggy steps right on top of me, but I somehow manage to locate my muscles, and I roll onto my side before the bulk of her weight can pin me. She jumps off me and bounces around in a circle near my feet.

I sit up, coughing and holding my chest. My lungs seem to have forgotten how to function. I wheeze in some air. Then I cough again.

"Mac? Are you okay?"

I look up, hacking into the foggy face of Joey Marino.

"Wow, you really do have goats."

I try to stand, but my lungs still can't figure out the inhale-exhale thing, so I drop back down on my knees and lean over, gasping for oxygen.

"MacKenna! Honey!" It's Coral's voice. "Coho, can you take her inside?"

I'm scooped off the grass and carried into the kitchen. Coho sets me onto a chair, then gets me a glass of water. He sits down across from me.

I gulp down the water. Every swallow brings a pulsing pain in my spine, but I'm not coughing anymore.

"These goats aren't your jam, huh, Mac?" Coho turns his head and gives me a sideways stare.

Finally, I can speak, but I sound more like a hamster than me. "That chicken you brought isn't exactly my jam either."

"I know." Coho nods his head and pushes the water glass toward me. "I feel your vibrations, MacKenna MacLeod. You're out of alignment with your core environment."

No, I'm not, I think. This man used to be aligned with me. We used to be on the same wavelength.

"Hank and Coral feel it too."

"Hank and Coral . . ." But I can't finish any thoughts on core alignment because Coral steps into the kitchen with Joey Marino right behind her.

"MacKenna." She leans down and hugs me gently. "Let

me look in your eyes. I need to see if you can focus." She puts her hands on my cheeks. "How do you feel now?"

"I'm fine." But I'm not really looking at Coral. I'm looking at Joey.

"Are you sure?" She brushes some straw off my shirt and pulls some grass strands out of my braid.

"I'm fine. Really."

Coral pats my cheek. "You didn't tell me this delightful boy was coming over this morning."

"Because I didn't know," I say, my voice still sounding hamster-like. But I give Joey a mammoth-size glare.

"Your house is right on my way to Sunnyville, so I just thought I'd stop." Joey turns to Coral. "Nice goats."

"They've been getting in the way a bit." Coral looks at me.

I don't know if she's referring to my fall or to the number of plants and pots they've kicked off her table.

"Joey, I'd love to hear more about the table scrap program you developed this year," Coral says.

"Sure, it was—"

"No, Joey can't stay," I say. "I mean . . . he's busy . . . at least, that's what he clued me into." I intentionally draw out the word *clue*.

Joey's eyes dart between me and Coral.

I stand up and grab his arm, my spine making an

instantaneous recovery. "Joey and I have to talk, Coral." I pull him into the living room, which he immediately scans from corner to corner, recording every detail in his brain: the incense pots; Hank's drums; the two futons, one on the floor, precise and structured, the other a heaping mess of flax-filled pillows and hemp sheets.

"Nice. It's big."

"You can stop all the brownnosing now," I whisper. "Coral's not here."

"I'm not brownnosing. You have a nice house."

"You're mocking it," I say. "Did you want a tour, because you've seen most of it. That mattress over there is my bedroom. There. You've now seen my world up close and personal. Happy?"

Joey is still, like I've just knocked him unconscious. He stares at his boots, and I do too. In the icy silence, the scuffs and the tears of his boots speak words that Joey has never spoken. Or words I've never listened to. Questions I've never asked. The pain in my back flares.

He wasn't mocking my house.

Or me.

I wish I could problem-solve people like I can a computer program. People don't always follow my steps. They jump out of the loops I've coded and create big ERROR messages in my head. Joey Marino more than anyone.

"I'm having a really bad morning," I finally say. And then the words just shoot out. "Hank thinks the new chicken is broody, but she's not, she's just . . . Satan in disguise. So now he wants to build her a new nesting box and a higher roost, and he's making me clean out the entire garage coop, and then help him build. I tried to tell him I was busy with my research, but he didn't listen. Which is pretty usual."

What does it matter if I just tell Joey Marino everything? He's seen my home life now. He's met my mom. Nothing should surprise him.

"Your parents don't know what you're doing, do they? They don't know about this hunt and the clues and prize money?"

I shake my head and put my finger over my lips.

"I won't tell them, Mac. I'll help you."

"Do you have a lead on one of the clues?" I whisper.

"No. I meant I'll help with the chicken, building a roost or cleaning or whatever."

"You don't have to do that. You should keep going on the hunt, visiting carts. I know that shot-in-the-dark clue is a coffee cart."

"Yes, but the sooner we finish, the sooner we can get back to the hunt. Together."

"Really?"

Joey sticks his hand out. I grab it and we shake again, like yesterday.

Together. Me and Joey Marino.

We're still a team.

We'll fix the broody chicken, and then we'll finish the food cart treasure hunt.

Chapter Twenty-Eight

Hannah and Isabel

Even with Joey's help, yesterday was wasted on Hank's broody chicken. Today, we need every moment to find the final two clues before tomorrow's deadline.

I arrive at the school playground exactly at eight a.m. like we planned. Joey's already here, squatting down near a woman who's leaning against a big oak next to the play structure. A loaded grocery cart is parked nearby.

I decide not to approach. This woman might be one of Joey's contacts. I don't want her to run away like the woman did when I stormed to Joey's rescue a few days back.

I sit down on a bench painted in primary colors. I wait and watch Joey and the woman.

I realize I've seen her before. She's the one Joey spoke to at the Hawthorne carts. She looks old, maybe seventy or more. Joey hands the woman a blanket out of the grocery cart. I've always ignored this woman. I've never considered giving her a warm drink or one of my rare spare coins, or even a hello. I've never wondered a thing about her.

But now I start to wonder a lot.

How long has she been homeless?

Where does she sleep at night?

Does she have enough to eat?

Should I give her my extra coat, the one I never wear because it's way too big?

Joey turns around and sees me on the bench. He says a few more things to the woman, and then he waves to her and smiles before sitting down next to me.

"Is she okay?" I ask.

"I think so."

"I was wondering if she might want a coat of mine."

Joey looks at me. He appears surprised by my question. I am too, a little. "You can ask her." He pushes on my back to make me go.

Slowly, I move toward the woman.

"Her name is Hannah," Joey says.

Gray-haired Hannah watches me intently as I get nearer. I wonder if she's fearful of people, fearful of everything, for that matter. It seems like you'd be hypervigilant if you lived outdoors all the time. I know I would be.

I clear my throat. "Hannah? I'm Mac. I'm a friend of Joey's."

Well, maybe I'm a friend.

"The hunt girl," Hannah says, her voice raspy, like an old blues singer's.

"Yes, I guess. I was wondering if you needed a new coat. It's not really brand-new, but I have one that I don't wear, and if you'd like it, I'll bring it to you."

Hannah's face warms, and some pink flows into her cheeks. Now I can see that she isn't as old as I thought.

"Joey told me you had a good soul," she says.

I blink. Joey Marino said that? About me?

"Can I bring it to you?"

"I can't pay for it." Her words crackle. They're worn down, like the life she's likely lived.

"I don't need any money," I tell her, even though that isn't exactly a true statement. "It's yours."

Hannah's gaze reaches inside me and touches me, like she's doing heart surgery with her eyes, and it's alarming how good it makes me feel . . . to give a coat away . . . to see her smile.

I return to the bench, but before I even sit down, Joey says, "Hannah saw my mom yesterday."

"Your mom . . ."

"Isabel. My mom Isabel."

"What do you mean? How would Hannah see your mom? Does she know her?" I ask.

Joey nods. "Remember the other day when I gave a book to the woman near the bank, and you chased her off, thinking you were rescuing me?"

I stare at him.

"That was Isabel. She's my mom."

What?

"That woman was your mom? I—"

I didn't know what else I should say.

"She seemed nice."

What a ridiculous comment. I could slap myself right now.

Joey lets out a short laugh. "Sometimes she's nice. Sometimes not. I never really know." He sweeps the hair from his eyes.

I absorb this all and try to sort it into the most logical programming sequence.

One of Joey's moms is sick.

And she's homeless.

So many questions swirl in my head, like for how long? And where does she stay? And does anyone else know? But the only question that comes out of my mouth is "Why?"

And Joey asks me in his sage-like voice, "Did you know that an estimated twenty-five percent of homeless people are mentally ill, Mac?"

I did not.

Joey sounds like a teacher, reading from a textbook.

"My mom is one of those. She's sick. She's not medicated, and she's on the streets."

I shift on the bench to face him. "What happened to her?"

Joey looks down at the dirt for a long moment. "Isabel used to be totally fine. She was even getting her law practice started. Then, when I was three, Ma told me things began changing. Isabel started thinking the landlord was listening in on her phone calls. She freaked out and would panic every time the phone rang. She wouldn't let Ma answer it. Then she would see things, like rabid dogs and bears. She swore the government was sending them to warn her of evil. She even accused Ma of being in on it, and that's when she left the first time."

I listen to his story. I want it to be fiction, just a creepy story, where adults assure you this would never, ever really happen. But Joey's eyes tell me it's real. Very real. He's lived it.

"Ma got her a doctor and they tried to get her to take some pills to help, and for a while she got better. This was when I was six, I think. Then one day she said she didn't need her pills anymore because she was fine, and about a week later she left again."

"She's been gone since you were six?" I ask.

I saw Coral riding her bike naked when I was six. I thought it was weird. Joey watched his mom leave their home at six. That's worse.

Way worse.

Joey slowly nods. "Ma tracked her down over and over for the first five years. She'd get Isabel home for a few weeks and try to get her to take the pills again, but Isabel refused, and she would just run off again. Ma kind of gave up. She couldn't do it anymore. So, I'm trying now. I want Isabel to be okay. Mostly, I want her to be safe."

I feel myself quivering so much I think I can hear my bones rattle. How does Joey keep going?

"When you see her out on the streets, does she know who you are?" I ask.

"I don't think so, but sometimes she looks at me really deep, you know? And then I wonder if she's remembering . . . something."

Isabel.

I remember how she grabbed Joey downtown a few days ago, how she mumbled a lot.

"Are you ever . . ." But I can't get the question out.

"Scared of her?" Joey finishes for me.

I nod.

"Yes." But Joey doesn't explain, and I don't ask him to. He wipes at his eye.

Then something occurs to me. "That's the reason you talk to so many homeless people, isn't it? Because of Isabel. Do they know her?"

"Some do."

"So, they help you track her and stuff?"

"Yes." He swings his boots under the bench.

Joey's story buries me. It weighs on me like concrete blocks. His mother lives on the streets, and he talks about it like it's ordinary, a part of anyone's world. Chickens and goats in my backyard seem so trivial. Stale, sugarless bran muffins for breakfast seem like a five-star meal. The blocks feel heavier. Hank and Coral give me a roof over my head. They live under that roof with me. I can't complain about that.

"Joey, I'm really sorry. I had no idea."

It's embarrassing how much stuff I don't know. First Brie and how much she really hates swimming. Then Willa and her dad's girlfriend and her parents' divorce, and now Joey and his homeless mother.

"It is what it is." He shrugs and turns away from me.

"It's kind of a lot to live with."

"Yeah, well, I don't think any life is perfect." Joey draws a circle with his toe in the dirt. He adds two dots for eyes, one for a nose, and a straight line for a mouth. "Everyone's life is a little bit broken."

Chapter Twenty-Nine

Mississippi Avenue

Joey rises from the bench. "Come on."

We walk away from the school playground, and I can see Hannah trudging along the sidewalk ahead of us, pushing her grocery cart.

"Yesterday, when we were cleaning the chicken coop, you told me you wanted to go to Mississippi Avenue. It's going to take two bus rides," he says. "So, let's go."

I look at Joey closer. I don't think he's even combed his hair. There're two cowlicks near his part. His gray T-shirt has a stain on the neckline. It's like I'm seeing him for the first time, paying attention for a change, noticing the broken pieces of him.

We step onto the 15 bus and find a seat near the front. Joey takes the window spot.

"What did Hannah tell you about Isabel? Where did she see her?" I settle in next to him.

Joey puts his backpack on the floor between his boots. It's bulkier than usual today. "Hannah said she was in Cathedral Park. Isabel was hallucinating, saying something about the St. Johns Bridge and how the light people would be there in two days."

"The light people?"

"Don't try to understand. It's not rational," Joey says.

But to me, it seems like Joey's trying to understand. I can almost hear the gears in his head clicking, sorting it all out.

I don't know if I should be discussing this with him. Does he want to talk about it? Does he want my help? Should I ask more questions? I don't have Joey Marino figured out.

Not at all.

But I understand where his head's at. As weird as my kale-wearing mother and chicken-loving father are to me, if either of them were living on the streets, I'd be worried about them too.

Every day.

"We have to find the last two clues, Mac. We have to."

For the first time, I completely realize how much this prize money means to Joey, and I refocus my thoughts on the clues and decoding once again.

I pull out my hunt folder and show him the list of carts. Two nights ago, I had highlighted all the coffee and breakfast carts. "I'm almost certain the shot-in-the-dark clue is at one of these. A shot is espresso, don't you think?"

Joey scans the list.

I rattle on about my theories. "Large is probably the size we need, and whole must refer to something on the menu."

"Whole bean?" Joey suggests.

"Or possibly the cart name."

Almost thirty minutes later, we hop off the second bus at the Albina and Fremont stop, then walk a block to Mississippi.

The hipster population has pretty much taken over Mississippi Avenue. Apartment buildings have been remodeled and painted funky shades of teal and eggplant. Diners have turned into vegan cafés. Bike lanes were added, and parking spaces eliminated.

I point across the street. "Come on. There's a taco place. I think we have to check out every cart we find to see if anything matches one of our possible clues."

But the menu at this cart shows nothing of interest, so we move on, past a bookstore and Mississippi Pizza, where people sit outside and drink their microbrews.

Two more blocks up the street, and we arrive at a pod of food carts.

I'll never get tired of the aroma around carts. This pod fills the air with scents of cinnamon and roasted garlic. There's a bright yellow trailer serving egg sandwiches.

Another cart serving ramen. One serves ribs and brisket with a smoker behind it that emanates a cloud of nostril-pleasing fumes. At almost every cart, there're long lines of people waiting, even though it's well before lunchtime.

"What do you think?" Joey asks.

I'm still checking everything out. One cart claims to have the best Southern food in town. I sniff the deep-fried grease smell and realize I'm starving.

The final cart in the pod is tucked behind a Korean place, so Joey and I move in that direction. The sign nailed to the top of the trailer says *New Orleans' Finest*.

And the sign's painted in green, gold, and purple.

I gaze at it.

Green. Gold. And purple.

I yank on Joey's elbow and pull him toward the New Orleans cart. The line is eight people deep. One couple carefully studies the menu board, which is just a bunch of photos of the food they serve. I pull out a napkin from my folder, the one with the clue about green, gold, and purple spices and shrimpy legs. I hold it open in front of Joey. "This is the cart!"

Joey quickly presses my arm down and whispers, "What do you think we order?"

We shift around the line of people, so we have a view of the menu. The clue repeats in my head: *Green, gold, and purple spices might get your arm strong. Shrimpy legs won't let you dance, but you can sing a song.*

Joey and I nearly knock our heads together because we both see it at the same time: Louis Armstrong shrimp gumbo.

Arm strong. Another sneaky clue.

I find myself thinking of Hank and Coral. They have vinyls of Louis Armstrong. They sometimes play him at night when I'm already in bed.

Joey taps my shoulder. "What about the drink?"

I glance through the list of beverages, which are the only menu items not pictured. There's the usual soft drinks, juices, and bottled water; but at the end of the list I see it: Mardi Gras sweet tea.

That must be it.

I pump my fist. The ninth clue could be waiting for us right inside that New Orleans food cart. Maybe it will be written on a paper cup or on the gumbo bowl. I don't care because it will be mine and Joey's just as soon as we buy . . .

An entire dictionary of swear words rises in my throat, and it takes the strongest lock around my impulses to keep those words from bursting out of me. How are we going to pay for it? I still have just four dollars and fifteen cents.

I yank out my flipper and check the time.

10:56.

I know what we need to do, but the thought of several hours of work makes me cringe. Inside, I'm still swearing.

I curse my four measly bucks, my lack of allowance, the hours Joey and I spent yesterday remodeling the chicken coop with no monetary compensation.

"How long do you think we'll have to work to earn the gumbo?" I ask.

Joey's looking around the pod in every direction. "It's really crowded here." He shakes his head at me. "We're not working."

"We're not? Do you have money?"

He shakes his head.

"What are we going to do, make a sign and beg for the money?"

I regret my words instantly.

Joey snarls at me. "I don't beg, Mac, but I also don't judge people who do."

His stone-gray glare shrinks me to a millimeter.

I do judge. All the time. Something else I'm not proud of.

Joey turns and walks away from me, and I don't blame him.

I watch him as he leaves the pod and returns to the sidewalk on Mississippi Avenue. He sits right on the curb and crosses his legs with his back to the street. He slides off his backpack and pulls out a case. It's a . . .

Ukulele?

Gently, he takes out the tiny instrument but keeps the case open in front of his legs. Then without tuning his strings, he starts playing. His right hand strums up and down; his left hand holds down the chords. And then he starts humming softly, but it's nice. It's mellow and folksy, like Hank, Coral, and Coho would love.

I stare at him and try to lift my jaw off the sidewalk.

He's a boy chameleon, changing with the environment to meet whatever need is right in front of him.

I glance around to see if anyone else notices him, seeing him the way I do, for the first time without any judgment.

A woman with about four scarves around her neck drops a dollar bill into Joey's open ukulele case.

Joey gives me a small wink. He keeps strumming and humming.

I continue to stand there, staring at him.

Joey's playing his instrument for spare change, and he doesn't even look . . . uncomfortable.

Another dollar drops in the case, followed by some loose change.

I move a little closer to him. More coins are tossed in the case.

I decide it's time to get over myself, so I sit on the cement next to Joey, crossing my legs like him. Our knees touch.

It's a real "Kumbaya" moment.

Joey Marino is brilliant.

Two more dollars are added into the case.

Joey Marino's spectacularly brilliant.

I find myself tapping my legs, pretending I have one of Hank's drums.

We keep going like that, strumming, humming, and tapping for about twenty minutes more, until the money total in Joey's ukulele case is over twelve dollars.

Enough for gumbo and tea.

I give Joey a firm nod and he clearly understands. He strums three more chords, hanging on to the last one to signal the end of our performance to the passing-by audience. A little girl in a stroller claps for us.

I scoop out all the money so Joey can put his instrument away. "Hungry?" he asks.

And I am.

I'm starving, in fact.

And I'm ready to get that clue.

I cross my fingers as we wait in line, desperately hoping that this will be a new clue, and not a duplicate of one we already have.

The shrimp gumbo is trickling over the sides of the bowl when it arrives. I discover the clue printed on the bottom of the bowl, and I carefully lift it up and peek underneath to read the words:

Burgers, sausages, chickens no way!
The sun shines bright, not just in the day.

Chapter Thirty

Details

"Mac! We don't have this clue. This is number nine!" Joey beams.

I've never seen him emit such enthusiasm. Joey Marino is one calm customer.

"Okay, Clue Genius, what do you think this means?" he asks.

The compliment shoots renewed energy through every blood vessel in my system.

I pull my hunt folder out of my shoulder bag and take out a blank piece of paper and a pen. "I think of this hunt like a computer program. I'll make a flowchart for you." At the top of the paper I write *Food Cart Clue Hunt*. "There are ten clues and ten carts, so each clue and cart are like one step of the code, right? But each clue leads specifically to another cart and clue, and it doesn't matter where you start, so it's not linear—it's really a big loop."

I draw a large circle and add ten dots, evenly spaced, around the rim. Then I label the dots on the path in sequence, beginning with Lorenzo's cart where I started, the double-decker bus, Oasis, the smoothie cart, and the New Orleans cart. Then I put a star by the first four carts indicating we'd solved those clues.

"Our problem is that we have five additional clues, and they all fall in this path somewhere." I point to the blank dots on my circle. "We just don't know what order they go in, which makes it hard to know which one to focus on to find the final cart and clue."

"Right," says Joey, "except we know that the shot-in-the-dark clue came from the grilled cheese cart."

"True. We can focus on just these four clues." I lay out the creamy-spicy-and-sweet clue, the one-meat-one-fruit clue, the shot-in-the-dark clue, and then our new burger-sausage-chicken clue.

Next, I draw an arrow by the dot right before Lorenzo's cart in the big loop. "This is the clue we need to find, the one that leads to his pizza cart. I ordered a meat combo pizza and a Coke to get that clue. None of these four clues seem like they would take us to Lorenzo's."

"So, what do we do?" Joey asks.

My phone buzzes.

It's a text from Willa: Call me.

My heart flips in a good way. I've been waiting for this text.

I push the circle diagram and the shrimp gumbo toward Joey. "Give me a minute. I've got to call Willa."

She picks up after only one ring. "Mac."

"You okay?"

Willa doesn't bother answering. "Sorry I've been quiet. Brie says you're still hunting?"

"Yeah. Actually, Joey and I just found the ninth clue." I look toward Joey and give him a slight smile.

"You heard that I'm going to move? Mom wants out of our house."

"Yeah, Brie told me. What about school?"

Willa doesn't answer right away. "I probably won't go to Winterhill."

I can't process that right now. I figure she can't either.

"I'm sorry about everything, Willa. You could have told me, you know?"

Joey's doodling around my hunt flowchart, but he looks up at me when I say that.

"Yeah. I know." She pauses. "I'm trying really hard not to be furious at my dad."

"I'm sorry," I say again.

"Anyway," Willa says, "I've got some time now, and I want to stop thinking about this divorce. Need some hunt help?"

"Wait. Seriously?"

"Yes."

"You think Brie can help too?"

"I'll ask," Willa says.

I instantly know what we must do. With four unsolved clues and four hunters, clue number ten is practically at our fingertips.

I snap my phone shut and say to Joey, "Let's catch a bus. We're going to find that last clue."

My thoughts churn with details of the nine clues; with Willa moving to a new school; with the hunt deadline looming; with Joey Marino and his mom, Isabel, on the streets, raving about light people.

We board the bus and Joey says, "You know if Willa and Brie help and we finish this hunt, we'll have to split the money four ways. Is that enough for your computer camp?"

"It'll be close. The camp's five hundred dollars, but I owe people some money." I think mostly of Coho and the money I stole. "What about for you? You never actually told me what you would do with your part of the money. You just said it was for your mom."

Joey slips his hand into an outside pocket of his backpack and hands me a brochure. On the front is a photo of a plain ranch house, painted in lilac. "This is Laurie's House. It's a transition house," he tells me, opening the brochure.

"I've checked out a bunch of these online and talked to Aggie." He points back to the title on the front page of the brochure. "Laurie's House helps people with mental illness who need to get off the streets. They offer medical care, counseling, job-seeking assistance, and more."

I hold the brochure, and unfold it section by section, glancing at the other photos, skimming the words.

"I need enough money for a deposit for Isabel to stay there, and then anything left over can go to medical treatment for her."

I look at Joey's eyes, the stone-gray eyes that match his mother's. Joey seems so much more like a parent than a son. It's so unfair that a twelve-year-old would have to do this for his parent. "But how will you get her to live there? Will she even go?"

Joey grabs the brochure from my hand.

Clearly, I asked the wrong questions, but I was trying. I really was.

Maybe Joey and I aren't the best teammates.

"If I don't get this money," he says, "Isabel stays on the streets, hungry and ill. I keep searching for her. Ma continues working sixty hours a week. Nothing changes." He shoves the brochure back into the pocket of his pack and scoots toward the window, away from me.

"If I have the money, I have some hope." His voice is a stirred-up mixture of sad and angry.

I wait for the angry part to come out, the part where he shouts, "Get it, Mac?"

But that part doesn't come. So, I say it instead, but in a whisper: "I get it."

I've shrunk to the size of a pea.

A mushy pea.

Chapter Thirty-One

The Team of Four

Joey and I meet Willa and Brie back at the Sunnyville playground.

It seems like my whole body lightens when I see my friends. They're leaning side by side against the monkey bars, and they look okay. Willa sees me first and she pirouettes toward me, takes my hand, and spins me in a circle before giving me hug. It's good to see her dancing.

They wave politely to Joey, as though he's always been around us and not just a phantom, and we all sit together on the grass. I pull out the four unsolved clues, handing one to each of them.

Willa reads hers aloud. "'Burgers, sausages, chickens, no way. The sun shines bright, not just in the day.'" She sets the clue down. "I have no idea what this means."

That's the one we got today. "I think it's a vegetarian or vegan cart," I say.

"I don't want to spend money on vegan food," Willa says.

Brie bumps Willa with her good arm. "Here. We'll trade."

Willa reads her new clue. "'Creamy, spicy, and sweet. Let them eat! Sip very slow, and then find the beat.'" Willa raises her arms and bobs her shoulders. "This is more like it. I can find a beat, but I have no idea what this means either."

"I have some thoughts on that one." I point at her clue. "I'm thinking it's a dessert cart. Joey has a clue that we're pretty sure leads to a coffee cart, and I have this one. It says, 'One meat, one fruit. Can you find the mate? It just might come from a small red state.'"

"These are tough, Mac," Brie says.

"I know. That's why we all need to work together. One of these leads to the final clue." I glance at my little flipper. "It's three o'clock. We have several hours left today until the carts close, and we have all day tomorrow, but that's it. First, I think we need to do some serious internet work to find possible carts. Then the tricky part will be traveling to all of them, and then, of course, paying for the food."

Joey speaks for the first time since we've arrived at Sunnyville. "We also need to figure out where to take the clues once we have them all."

"True, but let's find the last clue before we worry about that." I look at my three teammates. "For the rest of today, we'll split up. Joey, maybe you can search a few pods and check in with your connections." I pause for a reaction, but all he does is nod. "Brie, you can be our research center. Stick by your laptop and look up carts, pods, addresses, and other leads as needed. Willa, you can track down dessert carts, and I'm going to tackle this new clue and try to decode it. We'll text each other to keep tabs on our progress. Keep your phones charged."

I give all my teammates a thumbs-up and hope they're ready for this.

Willa reaches into her back pocket and pulls out a small wallet. She hands each of us a twenty-dollar bill. I attempt to rein in my bulging eyeballs. "Divorce guilt money from my dad," she says. "I might be getting a lot of this for a while."

"Thanks, Willa," Joey says. "And I'm sorry about your parents."

"You're the best, Willa," I add.

"Before we start," Brie says, "I should tell you guys something. I told my parents I'm quitting. I'm not swimming anymore."

I feel the corners of my mouth stretch from one edge of my face to the other. Brie told her parents the truth. And if Brie Vo can do that, then so can I. I can tell Hank and Coral that my future doesn't include chickens and goats, and rainwater collection systems, and recycled CD-case chandeliers, and public nakedness. I want a different life that will probably include a lot of beautiful technology. I need Hank and Coral to understand me.

"What did they say?" I ask.

"They said no. They said my shoulder would heal, that I have too much talent to waste."

"And?" Willa prods.

"I told them that maybe I could try something new. There's a cross-country team I could join, and I've always wanted to play soccer. It looks fun. Swimming all year has never let me do anything else."

"What'd they say to that?" I ask.

"They didn't like it. Then I started bawling. But I wasn't crying to make them feel bad. I was crying because I feel like I let them down. They refused to talk about it anymore, but I think they heard me."

Brie tears up, and Willa rubs her back.

The four of us sit quietly for a while with our thoughts. Then Willa leaps up and says, "Come on! What are we waiting for? Out with our old lives, in with our new! Let's hunt!"

Those are words we can all agree with.

Chapter Thirty-Two

Texts

When I arrive home, I'm relieved to find that Hank and Coral aren't here, and I don't bother texting them to find out where they are. There's no time for that. I park myself on my futon island and open my hunt folder. I'd written down the three clues I gave to Willa, Brie, and Joey so I could study them all more.

Five minutes later, texts start buzzing in.

3:45 Brie: I'm home. Send me your research requests.

3:52 Willa: Mom is driving me to cart pods.

3:53 Me: Brie, search dessert carts and locations.

3:54 Brie: On it.

3:56 Me: And vegan carts too.

I read the clue I'm in charge of over and over. I need to figure this one out.

One meat, one fruit. Can you find the mate?
It might just come from a small red state.

I blend words together to see if I can make any links, but nothing makes sense.

4:06 Joey: Down on Powell. No coffee carts here.

4:10 Brie: Dessert carts: Pies All, Tarts Today, Pastries and Puffs, Bavarian Bakes.

4:11 Brie: French Finest, Ice Cream We Scream, Candy Corner.

4:13 Me: The name has to do with music.

4:15 Joey: Heading to Foster Road.

4:20 Brie: Jukebox Jellies?

4:21 Me: Probably not. Keep looking.

4:25 Willa: Mexican Mecca has delicious tacos.

4:28 Me: You're supposed to be searching, not eating.

4:30 Willa: I'm starving. They have shredded beef!

4:40 Brie: How about Le Rythme de Paris? Rythme means "beat" in French.

4:41 Me: YES YES YES!

4:43 Me: Where is the Paris cart?

4:44 Willa: Yes! I'm ready for some French dessert.

Between text reading, I keep studying the small state clue, but I can't make heads or tails of it. Hank and Coral still aren't home, so I decide to catch a bus and join Joey to search for coffee or vegan or vegetarian carts. I text him first.

5:05 Me: Any luck?

5:08 Brie: Can't find any info on the Paris cart.

5:11 Willa: Mom's still driving me around. Maybe I'll see it.

5:14 Joey: No luck.

5:15 Me: Meet you at the Foster Road carts.

5:18 Me: Brie, search carts with SUN in the title.

5:19 Brie: Working on it.

5:23 Me: Willa, did you find that Paris cart?

5:27 Willa: Not yet. Still hunting.

It takes me over an hour to get to Foster Road and 52nd Avenue, but when I arrive I see Joey Marino sitting at a picnic table in the middle of the cart pod. A person who might be homeless sits across from him. Maybe this man is one of Joey's connections. I stand there and watch them. Joey's talking to the man. His hands motion in the air.

6:38 Brie: Can't find anything with SUN.

Joey gets up and kicks his combat boots over the bench. He glances around the pod and spies me. I wave, and Joey walks toward me.

"Find out anything?" I ask him.

"No. Nothing. Sorry."

It seems like Joey is smiling at me, like I'm a friend he's happy to see.

"I'm starving. Wanna eat?" He holds up the twenty-dollar bill from Willa.

I'm starving too. I haven't eaten since the Armstrong gumbo earlier in the day. I know we both need to save our money, but surprisingly, two meals in one day with Joey Marino kind of sounds like a nice idea.

"What are you hungry for?"

"Chicken," Joey says.

"Really?"

I don't think I've ever seen Joey eat meat of any kind. His lunches are always fruit, and . . . well, not much. The mystery of Joey Marino never ends.

He leads me to a cart that serves only chicken sandwiches, each sandwich named after a chicken breed. Hank would be appalled by this cart, but I love it instantly. Just as I begin to scan the menu, my flipper vibrates.

7:01 Brie: I think I found it! Sunny Day Thai Vegan cart.

7:02 Brie: But it closed at 7:00.

And then . . .

7:03 Willa: We found the Paris cart!

"Joey, look." I hold up my phone so he can read the texts. We pump our fists. At the same time.

MacKenna MacLeod and Joey Marino.

In sync for the first time ever.

I type a response back to Willa while Joey watches.

7:05 Me: What did you order?

7:06 Willa: Nothing. It's closed.

Joey and I sigh. Together. Still in sync.

We both look up at the chicken food cart. A man leans out the window and says to us, "Sorry, you two, we're closed for the day."

Sadly, all the food carts are in sync too.

Chapter Thirty-Three

The Rhode Island Red

Lying on my futon island in the morning on the final day of the food cart hunt, I tell myself that yesterday evening wasn't a waste of time. None of us found the final clue, but we made progress, and there's still a chance for us. We have two leads: the Paris cart that Willa and her mom found last night, and the Sunny Day Thai Vegan cart that Brie discovered. The small red state clue remains a mystery.

On the kitchen table, Coral has four large buckets, each filled with some water and those rhododendron leis she and Coho made the other day. She hugs me quickly. "Don't mess with these flowers, MacKenna. They need to stay fresh for tonight."

"Tonight?"

Coral gives me a curious look. "Yes, the bike ride is tonight. I told you, right?"

Bike ride? Flowered leis? This isn't another . . .

No. I'm not going to think about it. The hunt is all I should focus on.

I head out to the coop garage to face Poppy and the leghorn trio and grab their daily eggs. Ziggy, Marley, and Emmylou greet me with their usual goat swarming and prancing in circles. I don't understand why they have selected me as their favorite housemate. They need to go back before a neighbor complains and Hank and Coral get in trouble.

Slowly, I pull up the garage door, push the goats away, and keep my eyes alert for Poppy and a potential attack. She sits in her new nesting box like a prima donna.

Livie, Divie, and Bolivie perch on their roosts, like good, compliant hens. I gather three eggs from their empty nesting boxes.

"Thanks, you three." I actually speak aloud to them. Compared to Poppy, these chickens are okay.

Very slowly, I move toward Poppy. The goats follow me. She's not budging from the nest. She's securing her egg, like she has every morning since Coho brought her to us.

"You're too dumb to understand that your egg won't hatch no matter how long you sit on it," I say. "That egg is Hank's. You know Hank, the guy who loves you and drums for you, the guy who made you that new bed and roost."

I reach my hand out, staying calm, hoping that today will be different. "Be a good girl and move over. Let me have that egg."

But Poppy remains still. I inch my hand closer to her belly. My fingertips touch her, and I try to pry her off the egg, and that's when she attacks, drilling that needlelike beak into the back of my hand.

"Ugh!" I shake my pecked hand. "Why can't you be a nice, calm White Leghorn?" I scream at Poppy, like screaming will really help. Nothing will help me against her evilness. But I scream anyway. "You are a mean Rhode Island Red! You . . ."

I lower my injured hand to my side.

Poppy, the Rhode Island Red, is no longer glaring at me. Her crooked neck does some little side-to-side chicken jerks. She rises from her nesting box and steps out.

Rhode Island Red.

Small red state.

I can't believe it.

Poppy, the worst hen in the known history of my universe, may have given me the answer to the unsolved clue.

I snatch her egg and hold it up. "Poppy. Truce."

And I mean that.

Especially if it leads to clue number ten.

My mood has taken a U-turn, and I even pat each goat

on the head before returning to the kitchen.

Hank's already there when I enter. I hand him the basket. "These are going to be the best eggs you've ever had."

"Wow. You're in good spirits today, Mac. How are the hens?"

"Fantastic," I answer truthfully. "Especially Poppy."

"The cleaning and new nesting box must be what she needed." Hank pulls his eggs out of the basket and inspects each one.

Coral hugs me for the second time this morning. "MacKenna, I can sense your energies balancing. When are you going to tell us about your food cart research and what you're planning with all your findings?"

"This is the last day of my research, actually, and I . . . I was hoping I could talk to you both tonight."

I planned this when I got home from the carts yesterday. Brie telling her parents that she no longer wanted to swim inspired me to talk to Hank and Coral. I'm going to be honest with them, tell them that I don't want to always be part of their weird plans, their goat yoga, their drumming and guitar circles, their endless organic products they sell. I want to start living my life in a way that makes me happy, starting with the coding camp.

"I have the bike ride tonight, MacKenna, and Hank might join me too," Coral says.

"I don't know about that yet."

"Come on, Hank, it'll be fun! It's bonding, and it's for community awareness."

Coral can spin any event into a community cause. It's her gift.

"Anyway, will you tell me all about it tomorrow, honey?" Coral asks.

"Sure."

I absolutely will.

But first, my team and I must find the final clue and win the hunt, and this morning in the coop garage I got my lead.

I glance at the clock on my flipper phone.

Time to get rolling.

Chapter Thirty-Four

The Tenth Clue

Our plans are set. As soon as the carts open, Willa and Brie are heading to Le Rythme de Paris to figure out what to order, and I'm meeting Joey at the carts on Foster Road.

I don't tell Joey I've solved the clue. I want to see his face when I first let him know.

He's not at the pod when I get off the bus, but it's okay because it gives me time to study the menu at the chicken place, the exact cart we nearly ordered from the evening before. The Rhode Island Red sandwich is the third item listed. That just leaves me the question of what drink to order. Probably a fruit drink since the clue says "one meat, one fruit."

"I figured we'd go to a different pod today." Joey Marino appears right next to me, and I flinch. His black hair's in his eyes like always, his bottomless backpack on his shoulders. I'll never stop being amazed at his ghostlike moves.

"No. I wanted to meet here because you found the right cart last night." I grin.

Joey deserves the credit.

I hand him the clue and explain what we should order. I even tell him how I figured it out and show him this morning's stab wound from Poppy.

"I guess the new nesting box helped." Joey laughs.

And I like hearing that because Joey Marino doesn't laugh a whole lot, and laughter is healing. That's what Hank used to say when he was a laughter therapist.

"We just have one gamble," I say. "Do we order the lemonade, the limeade, or the raspberry-ade?" I reach for the twenty-dollar bill from Willa.

Joey whips off his backpack and sets it at his feet. "We're running out of time, so we order them all."

He crouches down and reaches deep into a side pocket. "I have Willa's money, and extra change in case we're wrong and have to buy more food somewhere else."

He's right. We do have to be sure. We must have this clue, and I'm filled with hope and a sudden belief that this *will be* a new clue, and not a repeat. This day feels lucky. The Poppy episode was merely the start.

I stride up to the counter of the trailer. "I'd like the Rhode Island Red sandwich, one lemonade, one limeade, and one raspberry-ade, please."

The man laughs. He takes my twenty and Joey's four

quarters and tells us he'll shout at us when it's ready.

"Where'd you get all that change?" I sit down at the picnic table across from Joey.

"Ma dumps all her diner tips in this jar in our kitchen. It's my lunch money during the school year," he explains. "But some days, I don't use it."

"Do you save it?"

"Kind of," he says. But then he lowers his head and doesn't say anything else, and I wonder if he's hiding some of his broken pieces from me.

"But then how do you pay for your lunch?"

Joey shrugs. "There's always fruit or other stuff on the free table at school."

The free food table. One of Joey's projects. It's where you put food you're not eating that someone else might want. I didn't think kids really ate that food. The free table is where I put most of the stuff Coral packs for me, and then I eat some of Willa's food because her mom packs enough for the whole class.

I wonder if Joey's eaten Coral's food. Her carrot salad? Her dry bran muffins? Her kale chips?

I'll probably never know for sure. I'm learning that he does things I've never imagined doing, because I've never needed to, or wanted to, or cared to.

Joey Marino's like an X-ray I haven't asked for, but that maybe I've really needed. And when I study the images from his X-ray, I see my insides, which show a person who thinks so much about all the weirdness in her own world she can't notice the people around her, living in their own worse-than-weird worlds.

"Your lunch is ready!" the guy from the chicken cart shouts.

Joey gets our food and brings it back to the table, sitting himself right next to me. The sandwich is wrapped in foil and underneath the sandwich is the receipt. On the receipt are two printed lines, and those lines are brand-new to me and Joey.

Pull on your boot, be adventurous too.
Try an animal combo of Classic and new.

It's the tenth and final clue.

Before I have time to process the words, Joey flings his arms around my neck and hugs me. Instinctively, my spine tenses, but somehow, I lift my arm, and rest it on Joey's back, hugging him too.

Joey releases himself from the hug first. "Mac! We have all ten clues. Now we just need to figure out where to take them. I'll go talk to the guy in the chicken cart. He might know."

Joey runs off, and I text Willa and Brie with the news: We found the tenth clue!

Joey walks back toward me shaking his head. The guy was no help. Joey sits back down, across from me this time. "I should . . . probably tell you something." His face still looks happy, but there's something serious in his tone. "I've known about this food cart hunt since it started. Hannah found out about it, and she told me about the prize money. I had four clues before you even started."

This should surprise me, but it doesn't.

"I wanted your help, Mac."

"My help? Why me?"

Joey folds and twists the foil from the chicken sandwich. "Because you're smart. Really smart."

Wait.

Joey really thinks that?

I always thought Mrs. Naberhaus was the only one who noticed my brain, and maybe Coho . . . but Joey does too?

"And also," he continues, "I thought you might want some extra money because—"

"Why didn't you just ask me to help?"

"What would you have said?"

"I would have said . . ." I swallow away the truth. I would have thought Joey was weird. I would have said he was making it up. I might have even laughed.

"I was trying to figure out a way to talk to you and tell you about the hunt, and then I got kind of lucky," he continues. "On the last day of school, when I saw you, Brie, and Willa at the Hawthorne carts, huddled over that tissue paper, reading something, I knew it was a clue."

"You stole that clue from me."

"You left it on the table." Joey flicks his straw at me.

We smile at each other.

"And then it was just a matter of following you and seeing which carts you went to." He takes a slurp of his drink.

"I thought you were stalking me," I admit. "Every time I turned around, you were there, like when I had feathers in my hair, when we were on the same bus heading downtown—"

"When we both saw the naked bikers." Joey bursts out laughing, spitting out some lemonade. He wipes it off his chin.

"Stop laughing!"

But he doesn't stop. He reaches for a napkin and cleans off the table where his lemonade spewed.

"It was funny, Mac. I thought that's why you and Willa and Brie were there too."

I turn away from Joey. "My parents are never funny to me."

Last night, I felt like we made such a good team. We were in sync and on the same page, both needing to win this prize money. Now I just feel like he's laughing at me like everyone else at school. It seems like he was just using me.

Joey stands up. He's not laughing anymore. He scrunches

the foil around the chicken sandwich and shoves it into his backpack. I look up at him. He's fading again, returning to phantom boy, the one I never saw, and through all the grayness of him I realize what I just said. *My parents are never funny to me.*

Joey's parents are probably not funny to him either.

I should apologize, but my jaw trembles, and then Joey speaks. "I need this money, Mac. And now you'll get it too. You'll be able to go to that computer camp and become the world's best supercoder." He swings his backpack onto his shoulder. "I'm sorry I laughed about your mom. I can be a jerk sometimes."

My eyes lock on his face and the colorlessness of his skin, and I wonder if winning this money will make that change. If it will bring him some pale pigment of hope.

Joey Marino's not a jerk, and I admit for the first time, "I'm the one who's a jerk."

Chapter Thirty-Five

The Next Step

After I saw the naked bikers for the first time six years ago, Coral sat me down with her on the living room futon. I did not want to talk to her about what I had seen, but she insisted. She tried to explain what she was doing, how she was expressing herself, but I didn't understand. Her words tied knots inside my body. The more Coral talked, the tighter all the knots became. They pinched and pulled, and I squirmed and wiggled next to her. Finally, I just got up and ran to the garage to hang out with our chickens. Escaping seemed like the best way to loosen the gnarls. It seemed like the only way to end Coral's talk.

Maybe that's what Joey and I needed right then. Maybe we both had to get up and escape the awkward conversation tying knots inside us both.

Maybe he and I are in sync . . . in a weird way.

The next thing we had to figure out is what to do with

the ten clues. We need to turn them in somewhere to win the prize. We decide to go to the Belmont Library and use their computers. Two bus rides later, at 1:10 in the afternoon, we arrive at the library. The computers are all in use, so I put my name on the waiting list, and text Willa and Brie to tell them where we are, and to meet us if they can. When thirty minutes pass, a man stands up and leaves.

I sit in front of the open computer and Joey finds a chair and squeezes in between me and the woman sitting at the next computer. She huffs at us, but neither Joey nor I move.

"What exactly are we looking for?" Joey's side is pressed against my arm.

"Hints." I navigate to the Food Cart Association website. "I remember Lorenzo told me to look here."

It takes a couple of seconds for it to load, and when it does, I look at all the tabs along the top banner.

Joey points to the *News* tab. "Open that."

I click on it. "I've read this a few times and haven't found anything. Guess we can look again."

I scroll down, and Joey and I both read, silently.

Burger Barn now serves side salads.
Tandoori moves to Killingsworth Station.
Grandma Jenny's sets July menu.
Podster Leo rates the Piedmont Carts.

"These don't seem like hints," Joey whispers. "They're more like little news bullet points."

I agree, but I keep scrolling down the page.

Eugene catches food cart experience.
Left Bank is now called the "The Big Corner."
Peppers goes to Cathedral Park.

I pause for a moment.

Cathedral Park. Why does that seem familiar?

I feel Joey's arm tense, just slightly.

I shake my head and keep scrolling, moving the mouse with my fingers slowly as we read line after line of food cart news.

Captain's Chinese closes.
Fire! is new on the East Side.
Tamales are their trademark.

"This list goes on forever." I look at the time on the bottom of the monitor. It's 2:15.

Cart tours available.
PF's Pod opens in Beaverton.
The sun will depart, and the ride will start.

"Stop." Joey whispers right into my ear and touches the screen. "That's odd. What does that line have to do with the food carts?"

But I don't answer because something else seems strange to me. I scroll back up the news feed, returning to another line we'd already read. Then I go down. Then up again, then down again.

"What are you doing?"

"Checking something." I scroll up and down once more and then let go of the mouse. "Joey, there're different fonts."

"What are you talking about?"

I show him three lines: the one about Cathedral Park, the one about tamales, and finally the one about the sun departing. "These lines are typed in a different font."

"No, they're not."

"Yes, they are. These three lines are Calibri, and the other lines are all Arial."

Joey squints at the computer monitor. "They look so similar."

"It's the size. The lines in Arial are in size twelve, and the lines in Calibri are in thirteen. That way they look similar unless you're really paying attention."

Joey leans back in his chair. "You're a total computer nerd, Mac, and you're brilliant."

I remember thinking the exact same thing about him

yesterday on Mississippi Avenue, playing his ukulele for our food.

Joey Marino and I make a pretty good team, after all.

I grab a piece of scrap paper and a tiny pencil and scribble down the three Calibri lines from the news feed. "Hey, look at the first two lines," I whisper. "'Peppers goes to Cathedral Park. Tamales are their trademark.'"

Joey stares at the paper.

"They rhyme! This is *the* final clue! Don't you see? The cart Peppers is where we turn in all our clues. We have to order tamales. I wasn't expecting that, but it makes sense. And this line here"—I point to the note—"tells us *when* to turn them in. When the sun goes down!"

I'm about to burst, but Joey's not. He stares at the note with the three lines I wrote down.

What's wrong with him? We're going to win two thousand dollars!

He finally speaks. "Cathedral Park is right under the St. Johns Bridge."

"I know. It's a long way from here. We'll have to check the bus schedule."

But Joey is stone-like still, as though *he's* suddenly a long way from here. "What's wrong?" I ask him. "We figured it out."

"It's just that . . . remember how Hannah told me she

heard Isabel shouting about the light people and how they would be at the St. Johns Bridge?"

I don't like the look on Joey's face, the look he gets when he thinks of his mom. It takes him somewhere else, away from this hunt and the prize money.

"It was two days ago when she said that," he adds.

"Joey, stop. The light people aren't real. You said so yourself. This has nothing to do with your mom." I feel certain about that. "Don't go crazy on me."

He looks away. I see him swallow, hard.

"I . . . didn't mean that. It was a terrible thing to say. I'm sorry."

And I really, really am.

"Joey," I continue, "there are no light people. It's not rational. That's what you said the other day."

He remains silent and still.

I nudge his arm. "Come on. We're just hours away from the prize. You're doing this for Isabel, remember?"

He shifts in the chair. "You're right. It's a complete coincidence. I don't know what I'm thinking."

He stands up, but I grab his hand and squeeze it tight. "I do not think you're crazy."

"I don't know. Sometimes I think I might be."

Chapter Thirty-Six

Cathedral Park

As Joey and I leave the library, I text Willa and Brie. I want us all to go to Cathedral Park immediately, but Willa's mom refuses to let us ride the city bus that far. She tells us she'll take us in the evening, drop us off, and then return no later than ten to bring us home. Joey says no to the ride, that he'll get there himself, but I make him promise to be there by eight, and I text him four times on the drive over to be sure he hasn't veered off track.

Willa's mom drops us off at a roundabout near the river. I notice all the people lingering on the grass and the narrow dock, and I get a bad feeling. How many are here to turn in clues for the hunt?

I've never been to this park before. There's tons of leafy green trees and wide walking paths, and I understand right away why it's named "Cathedral." The St. Johns Bridge supports are towering, pointed arches like in a Gothic

Cathedral. Willa, Brie, and I walk toward a little amphi-theater to wait for Joey. I stare at the bridge, mesmerized by its beauty, the lights along the deck, the elegant towers connected by the swooping cables. A thought of Joey's mom pops into my head. Gazing at this bridge makes her visions of strange light people seem almost real.

But that's too weird of a thought.

Everything will be okay.

I'm sure of it.

The only thing here tonight of any importance is Peppers, where we'll order tamales and turn in all our clues.

"So, you guys, I have something to tell you." Brie says. "My parents agreed. They officially told me I could stop swimming."

"Really?" I reach out and squeeze her hand.

Brie smiles, but it's hard to tell what's underneath that smile, whether it's happiness or some sadness.

I'm about to ask when I hear the beeps and dings of bells. We all look toward the sound, but we only see Joey walking toward us. He looks different. His gray T-shirt looks clean. And he's combed his hair.

"Guess who's here," Joey says.

"Isabel?" I ask, slightly worried.

"Who's Isabel?" Willa says.

"Nope." He's laughing. "The naked bikers."

"Oh. No."

This. Could. Not. Be.

But it is. This is Coral's big bike ride, the one she's been talking about.

It's the yearly World Naked Bike Ride in the city of Portland.

How did I not put this all together?

Why do my weird parents continue to ruin every good moment of my life?

The bell sounds get louder. I have a flashback of all the riders at the Joan of Arc statue, posing for pictures. Coral and Coho covered only in kale. Coral on my bike.

And now they're here.

A naked peloton.

Coral's in the middle, riding my bike once again. Her dreadlocks are loose and draped in front of her chest, covering her top body parts. Around her waist is one of those rhododendron leis, cleverly wrapped to conceal other parts. Coho rides right alongside her.

I have no idea why I'm watching this. I put my hand up to block the view, but it doesn't work, because I see someone else.

It's Hank, toward the back of the pack.

My crazy, drumming, chicken-loving father has joined the naked bike ride too. Flowers cover his midsection.

And he wears nothing else.

Nothing else but sunglasses.

Why? Why? Why?

I feel nauseous. I dash to the amphitheater, hide behind a concrete wall, and crouch in a little ball to squeeze all my screams inside.

Now it all makes sense to me. The other day, one of Coral's biking friends mentioned Cathedral Park was the beginning of the ride. Her friend meant the naked bike ride. He even said there would be food carts here.

And then there was that line in the news feed from the food cart site. The line that said: *The sun will depart, and the ride will start.*

The food cart hunt ends at sundown right when the naked bike ride begins. Only with my rotten luck would these two events be linked. It makes me wonder if I'm forever handcuffed to Hank and Coral's weirdness.

Finally, I come out from behind the amphitheater wall.

Joey, Willa, and Brie all attempt to conceal their grins. It's easy for them to snicker. None of their parents is here, nearly naked.

"You know." Joey is the first to speak. "The World Naked Bike Ride is really a protest."

"Protesting clothes?" Willa can't contain her laughter anymore. It fills her up so much she doubles over, grabbing her belly.

"No," Joey says. "They're protesting the dependence on oil, and they're also standing up for cyclist safety."

I'm not shocked that the wise-beyond-his-years Joey Marino would know that. It's certainly reason enough for Coral to join in.

"I don't care if it's a protest. It's just . . . weird. It's embarrassing." I turn away from my friends and start marching down the path through Cathedral Park.

"Get over yourself!"

I hear Joey's words and spin back around to face them all. "What?" I throw out my hands.

For once, Joey's face isn't gray. I can almost see blood surging to his usually translucent cheeks. "I said, get over yourself." He's glaring at me. "So what if your parents ride their bikes naked. It doesn't matter, Mac. We're here to turn in clues and win the prize money, so just get over yourself."

Joey's words sound like glass shattering. They cut and sting when they hit me.

Willa and Brie don't budge. They look at Joey, then at me, then back at Joey, waiting for the next glass to break.

Hank and Coral have always been nagging bugs in the computer program of my life. I'm always having to troubleshoot with them. I'm always rewriting the code.

I wipe at my eyes and glance down the path, but the naked bikers are out of our view.

Joey Marino continues to glare at me.

I smooth my hair and my shirt, take a deep breath, and pull my thoughts together. Joey's right. I do need to get over myself. I need to remember why we're all here.

"Let's go find Peppers," I say quietly.

The four of us follow the park trail, moving in the same direction the naked bikers had ridden. The trail winds through the park, past the river and a boat dock, and then toward a large parking lot.

"Look!" Brie points. "There're three food carts."

Immediately, I notice the green trailer in the middle.

Peppers!

Our finish line.

"And there're the naked bikers." Willa gives me a worried look.

It's true. The riders are gathered on the grass. Their bicycles are flopped on the ground or leaning against nearby trees. Hank, Coral, and Coho are among them. But there's also a lot of clothed people in a crowd near the three carts.

Joey says exactly what's on my mind. "Are they all here to turn in clues?"

"Maybe they're all just here for the bike ride," Willa suggests. "Maybe they just haven't . . . you know, dressed down yet."

From my bag, I pull out our ten clues, and fan them out. My hands quiver. We are so close. "We have to work our way to the front of that crowd, so we can turn these in. The sun is going down. It's almost time." I hand the clues to Joey. "I think you should be the one to do it."

"No," Joey says, "we'll all go together."

We step toward Peppers when I hear a voice.

"MacKenna?"

It's Coral.

Couldn't she ignore me? Just this once? Like I'm trying to ignore her.

Coral stands, wraps a shawl around her waist (thankfully), and jogs toward us. Her dreads and the flowered lei hide her chest.

"Honey! What a surprise. Hello, Willa, Brie, and Joey too." Coral beams at all of us. "Why are you here?" Then she whispers, "You're all a little overdressed."

Willa giggles.

"The food carts," Joey answers promptly, and I nod in agreement.

"Of course, your research!"

Brie sends me an eyebrow-raising look.

"Coral!" Someone from the group hollers at her.

"Better go! Have fun, all of you. We'll talk later, honey. Oh, did you see Hank?"

"Um, yeah," I answer.

Unfortunately.

Coral flits back to the naked riders and taps Hank and Coho on their backs. They both wave at us.

Willa waves back. "This is so hilarious. They should do a naked dance together."

"No. They shouldn't," I say. "Let's just do what we came here for, okay?"

Joey's holding our ten clues that equal two thousand dollars.

But right then, I notice two familiar figures slowly moving toward the mob of clothed people at the order window of Peppers. It's Shaggy and Scarface, both wearing only boxer shorts.

"You guys, come on!" I say. "I know those two are in the hunt. We've got to squeeze our way to the front, whatever it takes."

I run, weaving through bicycles toward Peppers, avoiding eye contact with the naked bikers. Willa and Brie are right behind me, but Joey isn't. I spin around to figure out where he is. He's still standing where we were before, where we spoke with Coral. He's looking the other direction, toward the bicycle path and the St. Johns Bridge.

"Why's he just standing there?" Brie asks.

"Joey! Come on! Bring the clues," I yell.

And then he emits a piercing shriek. It's just one word, "Isabel!"

Chapter Thirty-Seven

The Light People

"Joey!"

I race to where he's dropped our winning clues on the grass. "Joey, stop!" He's now running toward the bridge.

"What's he doing?" Brie's right on my tail.

I scoop up all the clues and shove them at Brie. "Take these to Peppers. I'll go after Joey."

"Where's he going? What's going on, Mac?" Willa shouts, catching up with me and Brie.

"Just turn in the clues. Go! Hurry!"

I begin running after Joey, but he's way ahead. Then I have an idea. I double back to the naked gathering, toward Coral.

"I need my bike."

I give Coral no opportunity to answer. I just lift my bike off the grass, kick my leg over the seat, and struggle to pedal it through the grass. I wobble my way between the naked bikers and toward the paved path. I pedal hard and fast, feeling my thigh and calf muscles burning, trying not to lose sight of Joey.

The path curves near a small grove of trees. Just beyond that is the grassy clearing where we all met earlier, with the St. Johns Bridge towering in full view.

Joey's sprinting onto the grass, toward the bridge, and now I see another person in the distance.

It's Isabel.

"Joey!" I yell.

But he doesn't turn around. He just keeps running toward his mother until he's about ten feet away from her. I finally catch up to him and clench my bike brakes, stopping at his side.

We both stare at Isabel, our chests heaving.

"Light people. The light people," she mutters. "They're here at the bridge. The light people. I saw the light people. . . ." Isabel's eyes bulge. Her arms are spread wide, swaying back and forth as she rambles on and on.

I grab Joey's arm. I'm still straddled over my bike.

"It's okay, MacKenna. I've seen her like this before."

But something makes me uneasy.

Isabel looks like a wild animal lost in the middle of a city.

"Isabel?" Joey moves forward.

I hold his arm tighter. "Maybe you shouldn't talk to her."

"Light people are here. I see you. Light people are here. I see you." Isabel continues to ramble.

She's looking toward me and Joey, but not really at us. Her hair is Einstein wild, sticking up in all directions. Her wool coat has mud on the sleeves.

"Joey." I'm whispering now. My hands tremble. "I think we should back off and leave her alone."

But Joey ignores me. "Isabel?"

He takes another step forward. "Do you recognize me?"

"Light people! Light people!" Isabel yells now. She points her bony finger, but not at us.

Joey glances over his shoulder. "The bike riders?" Then he looks back at his mother. "Are those the light people?" He takes another step forward.

I no longer have hold of his arm.

"Isabel, I'm Joey. I bring you books and food. Do you recognize me?"

Isabel lowers her voice. Her words become incoherent, like a foreign tongue.

"Joey, please. Don't go closer. Let's get help." A warning light blinks in my head: ERROR. ERROR. ERROR.

But he still ignores me. He takes yet another step. "I'm not a light person, Isabel. I won't hurt you." He's close to her now, maybe just five feet away.

The lights from the bridge above us give Isabel an eerie halo. Her mutterings grow louder again. Her arms begin to flap up and down like wings. Her eyes glow as she stares at Joey.

"Isabel?" he says again.

And then Isabel screams, a long shrill note, her mouth wide, every tooth exposed.

I shoot forward on the bicycle and grab Joey's arm again, yanking hard to move him back, away from Isabel, but he's a rock. I can't budge him.

"HELP!" I holler, louder than I've ever yelled in my life. "HELP US!"

Isabel's scream doesn't stop. It drowns out my yells. It pierces my eardrums.

She reaches into her coat pocket, slowly at first. I watch every movement.

Then her hand jerks out of her pocket. Is she holding something? She swings her arm right at Joey.

Instinct, or maybe fear, takes over my muscles. I stomp on my bike pedal, charging at Isabel. The front tire slams into her knees, and she collapses to the grass in a heap, but her screams don't end.

I lose control of my bike and fall over too, right next to Isabel. She kicks her legs at me and the bike.

I hear another scream.

"No, Mac!"

What have I done?

I push on my bike frame, wiggling out from underneath

it, and jump to my feet.

Isabel's still on the grass, still screaming, her arms and legs wildly thrashing.

"Move away! Move away!" Four police officers rush toward us. They motion us to move back. Two of them stand close to Isabel, leaning over her. She keeps screaming.

Joey lunges toward the cops. "Don't hurt her. Please, don't hurt her."

A third officer holds Joey's shoulders and moves him back. Joey twists his arms, but the officer is incredibly calm. "You should stay back. We won't hurt her. We promise." He holds Joey tighter.

The fourth cop puts his hand on my shoulder. "Kid, are you all right? What do you think you were doing?"

I can only shake my head to answer because I can't find my voice. I step toward Joey and the cop who holds him. I take Joey's hand, and he stops shaking and twisting. The cop releases him, and he flings his arms around my neck and sobs. Every broken piece of Joey's life comes out with his tears and they land on my shoulders.

I put my arms on his back, and I hang on tight, trying to somehow glue him back together.

The cops next to Isabel are reaching out to her, talking to her. She's no longer twisting or jerking or screaming, but her mutterings begin again—light people coming, I see them . . . It goes on and on.

"Mac!"

I lift my head and see a crowd of people approaching. Joey still clings to me. I don't let go either.

Hank, Coral, and Coho are part of the crowd, and I don't even think about their public nakedness, because their expressions hold nothing but concern, the kind of concern any parent would have for their kid when that kid might be in danger.

Willa and Brie appear next. They rush to the front of the crowd. Brie hangs on to one of Willa's arms. Tears stream down her cheeks. Willa looks like she's been punched in the gut, which is how I feel too, but I keep hold of Joey, who's still trembling.

"Son," one of the cops asks, "do you know this woman?"

I feel Joey's head move, but he doesn't speak. So, I answer for him. "She's his mother. Her name is Isabel."

Chapter Thirty-Eight

The Food Cart Hunt Results

The two police officers near Isabel help her to her feet.

Joey finally lifts his head from my shoulder and lets go of me. "Wait." He wipes away tears. "What are you going to do with her?"

"We'll help her find a place to stay tonight."

"Not the Manor," Joey says. "She doesn't like the Manor. Take her somewhere in Southeast, please?"

"Light people! Light people!" Isabel yells. Her body shakes. The two cops hang on to her arms tightly. Her fingers flare out. The cops turn Isabel away so she's facing the bridge, and not the crowd of bikers. It calms her a little.

"Wait!" Joey walks toward the policemen. I follow him. "Will you contact me? Will you let me know where you take her?"

"Son, is there another adult we can contact?"

Joey nods and gives them Aggie's number. One of

them jots it down into a small spiral notebook. Everyone watches them walk away with Isabel. who still rambles on and on. We keep watching until they're completely out of view.

Most of the people wander back toward the parking lot, but Hank and Coral stay. I realize that someone has given them clothes. Hank wears a pair of shorts, and Coral has on a jacket that looks like Brie's.

I'm grateful for their sudden decency.

I pick my bicycle up off the grass and roll it forward to Coral.

She drops the bike on the ground and pulls me in for a hug. "MacKenna, are you okay?"

"Yes."

"You're filled with surprises tonight," Hank adds.

"Yeah," I say. "You too."

They both chuckle.

"How about you, sweetheart?" Coral peers at Joey. "Are you okay? What can we do to help you and your mom?"

Joey shakes his head. "Thank you. There's really nothing to do right now."

"Well," Hank says, "you kids want to join the bike ride?"

I have no idea what my face looks like right then, but Hank bursts out laughing. He slaps my back. "I'm kidding, Mac!"

Coral picks up my bicycle. "We're not doing the ride

either. We'll take the bus home with you." She hugs each of us once more.

"Willa's mom is going to drive us home," I say, and Willa nods in agreement.

Hank and Coral look at us all carefully, probably sizing up the energy surrounding us, determining whether we are balanced and turbulence-free.

"All right," Hank says. "We'll go tell Coho what's going on, and then we'll ride home and meet you there." He's looking right at me.

"Thanks," I say.

I stand there quietly with my three friends, watching my parents walk away. The lights of the St. Johns Bridge cast glowing beams on the grass.

Willa breaks our silence. "This night is intense!"

"No joke," Brie adds. "What were you two thinking?" She gapes at Joey and me.

"I was thinking of my mom," Joey answers. He drops onto the grass.

And I was thinking of Joey, but I don't say that out loud. I sit down next to him.

"So, now you both know my secret too. My mom is homeless, and, yes, I follow her, and I keep tabs on her, and I worry about her every day."

"What was she talking about, Joey? Light people?" Brie asks.

He shrugs. "It had to be the naked riders, but I don't get it. Somehow, she knew they would be here. Maybe they reminded her of something. She was seeing and thinking things that weren't there."

"Can she get better?" Brie says.

"Maybe, but not unless she gets help and meds and off the streets." His voice shakes.

Brie and Willa lower themselves to the grass. I know they're really seeing Joey now, not the phantom Joey, but the Joey who's real, who's now my friend. The four of us form a circle, knees touching. We sit in silence, the bridge lights illuminating our faces just enough.

"Hey!" Joey says. "The clues? What happened to them?"

"Well," Willa says, "we have good news and then less-than-good news."

Joey and I lean forward.

"Brie sprinted back to Peppers and slid right in front of the crowd, even ahead of those two guys in their boxers," Willa says.

"It wasn't that hard. When you screamed, Mac, everyone was distracted," Brie adds.

"Yeah, well, your foot speed was impressive," Willa says.

"Then what happened?" I urge them to tell us the rest.

"We ordered four tamales and gave them the ten clues," Willa continues. "They looked them all over, and then they had a third guy look at them."

"What did they tell you?" Joey asks.

Brie smiles. "They said, 'Congratulations. You are the first to turn in ten clues in the Portland Food Cart Association Treasure Hunt!'"

"YES!" I throw my fists into the air. Willa and Brie high-five me. "We did it! We actually won!"

I leap up. I feel like dancing like Willa always does, a victory dance. "This is really happening!"

Both Willa and Brie jump up too. We pump our palms together up in the air.

Joey gets up too, but he doesn't dance with us. He puts his arms around me and hugs me tight, but this time he's not crying like before. This time I feel the broken pieces in him mending, and when he lets go, I see something in his face that I'm not sure I've ever seen in Joey Marino.

I see color, a warm pinkness. Maybe it's from joy.

And maybe it's from hope too.

"We better tell them the rest, Willa."

Brie motions for Joey and me to sit back down.

"Well," Willa begins, "I did say that there was good news and then less-than-good news. The good news is that we turned in the clues first."

"Tell us the less than good," Joey says.

"The less than good is that there are two winners. They split up the prize money between us and your boxer shorts friends," Willa explains.

"Shaggy and Scarface?" I say. "But you turned them in first."

Brie shrugs. "I know. I was going to ask about that, but then the cops started charging toward the bridge, so Willa and I did too."

"So, it's not two thousand?" I ask.

Willa shakes her head. "Half. One thousand."

Brie reaches into her purse and pulls out an envelope. She hands it to me. On the front in green ink is written: *Food Cart Association Treasure Hunt, First Prize.*

I open it and count ten bills. I pull one out and feel the crispness of it in my fingertips. For the first time ever, I'm holding a one hundred dollar bill with the face of Benjamin Franklin.

I imagined there would be twice this many bills. I imagined that holding a piece of money this large would whisk me away from the weirdness of Hank and Coral, and lead me down a different path, toward becoming a supercoder, the path I was so sure I wanted just a few days ago.

But it doesn't.

I tuck the Franklin back into the envelope. "We'll have to break some of these bills so we can evenly split the money."

Brie takes the envelope out of my hand. "No. Willa and I aren't taking any. We already agreed on that. You and Joey did all the work and deserve all the money. It'll be easy to split."

She pulls out five bills and hands them to Joey, then gives the envelope back to me.

Joey shoves the money into his backpack. "Thanks."

I wonder what he's thinking.

I wonder if he's disappointed.

Because I am, even though it's exactly the amount I need for the coding camp.

I fold the envelope and slide it into my back pocket. "Thanks, Brie. Thanks, Willa."

"And . . ." Willa holds up a paper bag. "We have tamales!"

They both smile.

Willa and Brie.

My best friends.

Chapter Thirty-Nine

Parents

Willa's mom drops me off at home just after eleven p.m. I enter the front door, and Hank and Coral are waiting for me, both sitting on the futon couch. Hank softly taps on his drum, but he sets it aside when he sees me.

Coral pats the futon between her and Hank. I sit down and let her wrap her arms around me and nestle her plastic-filled dreadlocks in my face. "Oh, honey, this was an eventful evening."

I pull away from Coral just a tad, so I can see her face. "Yeah."

"I had no idea about Joey and his mom. I ache for them." Coral presses her palm to her heart.

"Joey has another mom too. Her name's Aggie and she works at Patsy's Diner."

Coral sighs. "We'll think of some way to help them."

I nod and let out a long exhale. "I should probably tell you about my research."

I fess up about the whole hunt, starting with how I stumbled upon the first clue at Lorenzo's, which led me to the double-decker bus cart. I tell them about the delicious tagine I ate downtown at Oasis, which led to the smoothie cart. I thank Coral for her help with that clue.

Hank and Coral listen patiently and don't interrupt, like the alternative Earth therapists they strive to be. I have their full attention.

Then I tell them about Willa's parents and their divorce, and how Willa's mom is selling the house, and they're moving.

Coral reaches out and grabs one of Hank's hands and one of mine. "Sometimes relationships fall out of sync, MacKenna, but Hank and I are forever. We want you to know that."

"You're not even married."

"We don't need to be." Hank smiles at Coral. "Willa and Becca will be okay."

I believe him. Willa's world of song and dance won't end with her parents' divorce.

Then I tell them about Brie, and how she sprained her shoulder and how that led to her admitting to her parents that she didn't want to swim anymore and how angry her parents got.

"Brie will find her path on our Earth. Just like you will."

Coral squeezes my hand. "We can feel how hard you're looking."

"You can?"

Have they really always known that? It's never felt like it to me. But they are smiling at me and listening to me, so I keep sharing, and I tell them about teaming up with Joey and learning about Isabel. I even mention all the clues that Joey got by talking to his homeless connections. Hank and Coral hang on to every word of my story, attuned, as Hank would say.

Hank and Coral love a good story.

Hank and Coral love a lot of things.

Finally, I tell them about finding out that the clues had to be turned in at a cart called Peppers, which was going to be at Cathedral Park.

"The start of the naked bike ride," Coral says.

"Yeah. I didn't figure that out until today."

"Were your friends embarrassed?" Coral asks.

My friends? I can't help but laugh.

"Mac." Hank holds both my wrists. His eyes are serious. "You were brave tonight."

I'm not sure about that. I acted out of pure fear. I thought Isabel was going to hurt Joey. I thought she had something in her hand, but she didn't, and I plowed her over with a bicycle.

That doesn't seem like bravery.

"So," Hank asks, releasing my wrists, "did you win the hunt?"

I smile, relieved by the change of subject. "We did, and we got a prize, one thousand dollars."

Coral gasps.

Hank pats me on the back. "What will you do with the money?"

I know exactly what I'm doing with the money, and I'm ready to confess everything, that I wanted the money for a computer coding camp, that I was planning to ask Coho to help me, that I even stole some money from him, but none of those words come out of my mouth because . . .

"Hey. Where's Coho?"

Hank and Coral look at one another. "Coho had to veer from us tonight. He's dealing with some unfinished business."

"He is?" I wonder if it has to do with his old job. Maybe he's going to return to it. Whatever it is, I owe him money, and I'm going to pay him back. That's the first thing I'm doing with my prize money.

Coral yawns. "How about we talk more in the morning? It's been a long night. We should all retire."

And I like that idea because it's almost midnight, and tomorrow's an important day.

Chapter Forty

Coho's Gift

I wake up at eight thirty the next morning, two hours later than usual. I lie on my futon island staring at my poster, *Girls Are Supercoders*. When this poster hung in Mrs. Naberhaus's classroom, I would look at it every day and whisper the words to myself, certain that the more I said them, the better chance they would become true for me. Someday.

But today when I whisper the words, they feel different on my tongue. Maybe it's because Joey Marino and I completed the treasure hunt. Maybe it's because I have five hundred dollars in the pocket of the jeans I wore yesterday. Maybe it's because I don't feel like the same MacKenna MacKensie MacLeod after last night.

Coral is still asleep, snoring her half of the morning duet, but Hank isn't there. I don't want to wake her. There's something I have to do first thing, right after I dress and braid my hair.

I slip out the front door and walk briskly to the little convenience store down our street. At the store, I break one of my Franklins into smaller bills.

When I return home, I go straight to the garage to feed the chickens and collect the morning eggs. I tiptoe through the straw bedding toward the chickens. I'm going to try a new approach this morning. "Sweet Poppy," I call.

The diva hen perches in her new nesting box. I grab the eggs laid by Livie, Divie, and Bolivie.

"Remember our truce, Poppy?"

I stretch my arm out to nudge her aside, and this time, she actually gets up and moves. Poppy, the former meanest hen in the world, moves off her nest without stabbing or skewering me.

She doesn't squawk at me either.

And . . .

She left two eggs.

I take them both at the same time, not quite believing what I'm holding. They're two perfect Poppy eggs. I gently place them in Coral's basket.

Poppy is a changed fowl. I almost want to pet her.

Heading back to the house, I sense something weird. The backyard is quiet, almost peaceful. It's a sensation I'm not used to.

Hank is beside himself when he sees the five eggs. "Will you look at that. I've heard about hens laying more than one egg in a day, but I've never seen it!" Hank lifts them all and inspects them closely. "This one has a slightly soft shell."

"Poppy laid two," I say. "I think she's done brooding."

"I knew she would come around."

"Yeah. She kind of did," I admit.

"I still think it was the goats," Hank says.

That's when it hits me. The stillness of the backyard. "Hank! The goats are gone. They must have got out."

"No." Coral enters the kitchen, yawning. "The goats went back."

"It's true," Hank adds. "Coho and I actually returned them yesterday. You were away most of the day, so you didn't know, and last night you were dealing with some unusual energy, so we didn't tell you."

"What about your goat yoga for the Earth Festival?" I ask.

"It will just be meditative yoga without goats," Hank explains. "I never sensed those goats were attuned to our frequencies."

I clear my throat and remind them, "They weren't legal either."

"Mmmm." Hank nods and sits at the table.

"The festival will still be colossal, Hank." Coral pats his hand.

Goat yoga is weird. The Earth Festival is weird, and so are my parents. And they aren't likely to change. If I've realized anything over the last few days, it's that I can deal with weirdness. I always have. There are some situations that are far worse, and I don't have to deal with those.

"I have to tell you both something." I reach into my pocket and pull out some bills, placing them on the table. "I owe Coho some money. I . . . um . . . I took thirteen dollars from him to help me with the hunt."

"You took money from Coho?" Hank asks.

"Yes. I'm sorry. I shouldn't have. I—"

"Coho left early this morning," Hank says.

"What do you mean he left? I thought he was staying for your festival."

"He said his path was pulling him, guiding him else-where." Hank exhales deeply, then he grabs the bills on the table. "I don't know where Coho's going, so I'm not sure how to get this back to him." Hank presses the bills into my hand. "I don't like what you've done, Mac, but I'll trust you to make a good choice with this."

I stare at the money in my hand.

"Coho left you something," Coral says.

"He did?"

"It's on our bed. You should go check it out."

After bringing us a chicken and some goats, it's a little frightening to think about what he might have left me.

But when I enter Hank and Coral's room, there's some-thing silver and rectangular on their mattress.

It's a . . . laptop computer.

I gently pick it up, and I smooth my palm over the front, the sides, the back. I open it and touch every key. The screen has some smudges. I'll clean those right away.

"He left this too." Hank hands me a large envelope.

I pull a note out of the envelope first and read Coho's words:

> *Mac,*
> *Our Earth often chooses our path, but then later guides us to a fork. I've hit a fork, and I'm trusting a new path. You're young. Stay on your path, but never be afraid of the forks.*
> *Coho*

Also, inside the envelope is a paperback booklet, *Learning Python: A Beginner's Manual.*

"Python?" Coral looks over my shoulder. "Hank and I knew you would love the computer, but I don't understand why he would leave you a manual on snakes."

I laugh so hard I flop over on the mattress, hugging the book to my chest. I'll try to explain what this means to Coral later.

I sit up. "You guys are really okay with me having my own computer and screen time? Because I do love this. So much." I touch the laptop again, gazing at its beauty.

Hank nods. "All in moderation so your energies remain level, Mac."

"Of course!" Even ten minutes a day on this computer learning a new coding language would be . . . colossal!

Coho still understood me. He may have changed into the Earth brother that Coral always longed for, but he still saw me.

Hank and Coral smile at me.

They see me too.

"So, Mac, I have a drumming circle starting in thirty minutes—want to join us?"

"Um . . ." My eyes bulge.

Hank slaps me on the back. "I'm kidding! I love you, Mac."

"I love you too, MacKenna," Coral adds.

I hold the laptop in my hands and feel my entire body deflate, as I exhale twelve years of self-inflicted parental mortification—the sopping-wet bicycle rides to school when I arrived drenched and my pants didn't dry until lunch—the Career Day where they both came to school and tried to do laughter therapy with my classmates—the naked bike rides—the chickens—the goat yoga—the bongo drumming.

Hank and Coral.

The weirdest parents in the world.

"Yeah," I say. "I love you both too."

Chapter Forty-One

Joey Marino

Sometime after breakfast, I get a text from Joey: Meet me at Sunnyville School.

I brush my teeth and redo my braid, making sure it's tight with no loose hairs.

Just before heading out the door, I remember something about the last time I met Joey at Sunnyville—a certain promise I'd made. I open the coat closet in the living room and dig deep into the back rack where I find my too-big winter coat. I shove it into my shoulder bag along with my new laptop and Python manual.

Joey's sitting on the same bench as before when I get to the playground. I wave at him, then look to the big oak in the center of the playground where the familiar figure I'm hoping to see is propped against the trunk, her grocery cart close by.

"Hannah?" I approach her. "It's Mac. We met a couple of days ago."

She looks up, her expression somewhat empty.

"I brought you a coat, like I said I would." I hold it out, and Hannah's eyes connect with mine.

She smiles, her lips curving in slow motion, and in her bluesy voice says, "Aren't you a kind old soul."

"The pockets are really warm." I wink at her. I don't mention that I've tucked the thirteen dollars that was supposed to be for Coho inside one pocket. Hannah can probably use a decent meal.

I think Coho would agree with me.

"Aren't you a kind old soul," Joey mocks when I sit down next to him, but he's grinning and his gray eyes sparkle. They almost look blue.

"I saw Isabel this morning," he says. "They took her to a shelter on Grand Avenue last night. Ma and I went to help with breakfast. I served her some pancakes and coffee."

"Really? Did she say anything to you? Anything about the light people? About getting hit by a bicycle?"

Joey laughs a little. "No, she was pretty quiet and hungry."

"I'm sorry we didn't get all the money from the hunt, Joey."

He shrugs. "I gave my prize money to Ma and told her what it was for," Joey says. "She told me that maybe we could save all her tips during the summer and then we might have enough for the Laurie's House deposit by fall."

"Don't you need her tips for other things?"

"I have lots of ideas for getting things without money."

That's true. I've been part of his ideas over the last few days.

There's no one I know who's quite as resourceful as Joey Marino.

"What about you? Did you sign up for the camp?"

I don't answer him. I pull out the prize money envelope from my pocket, where I've had it since early this morning. I hand it to Joey. "There's four hundred and eighty-seven dollars in here. I took out some money I owed," I say. "Will that be enough for the deposit?"

Joey stares at the envelope and then right into my eyes. "You're giving this to me?"

"Well, I suppose it's really for Isabel."

He opens the envelope and thumbs through the bills. "The deposit is eight hundred dollars."

"Then the rest can be for her medicine or something."

Joey closes the envelope. "But this is almost enough for your camp. I'm sure Mrs. Naberhaus would let you pay the rest later."

"It's probably full now. There were only two slots left anyway, and . . . I really want you to have it."

Joey's eyes fill with tears, and his cheeks lighten. It's like the gray ghostliness of Joey Marino has completely vanished.

"You said that Laurie's House might be her best chance.

257

Isabel deserves a chance," I say, and I mean it, but I also think Joey deserves a chance.

"Thank you." His voice is barely a whisper. And I'm sure he's wondering all kinds of things, like whether they can get Isabel to go, and whether she'll stay, and whether she'll have good days again. But those are all unknowns. All he can do is plan the program, run it, and see what happens. There's always troubleshooting in computer programs. It's really just like living. Energies change, as Hank and Coral would say.

Joey takes a big inhale, then reaches down to dust off his combat boots. "Thank you, Mac," he says once more.

"Actually, I should be thanking you."

Joey eyes me.

"For making me a better friend," I say. It's really true. And I'm going to keep working at it . . . being a better friend to everyone . . . Willa. Brie. Joey.

"You know, even though the food cart hunt is over, maybe we can still hang out this summer. Maybe we can team up on a different project."

Joey leans on the backrest and tilts his head, like he's calculating all my past actions, adding them up to see if he can believe me.

"I'm serious," I say. "Hey, let me show you something." I pull out my new laptop and set it on Joey's lap. "Coho gave it to me, and this." I pull out the Python manual.

Joey opens the laptop and touches the keys exactly like I had. "He just gave it to you?"

"He's following a fork on his path."

Joey squints at me. "What?"

I elbow him lightly. "Things aren't always rational around my house."

"Yeah. Goat yoga's kind of a strange path." He laughs and elbows me back. "Wait until that gets around."

"Too late. The goats went back. Had the wrong frequencies."

He lifts an eyebrow. "Weird."

"Don't I know it."

Joey rubs his palms on his thighs. "Thanks for helping me with the hunt, Mac, but you don't have to keep helping me."

His words sting, and I look away from him and focus my eyes on the smoothness of my laptop, rebooting my thoughts. "I just figured that community projects are your thing, and computer programming is kind of mine. Between the two of us, there must be something cool we can do. Maybe we could see if the food carts are donating their leftover food to the shelters around the city. I could write an algorithm for which shelters like which carts."

Joey squints at me like he's still not sure of my ideas, or me.

"But we could also just help at some shelters, serving

meals or collecting clothing. Maybe they need help at Laurie's House."

"That's good." Joey finally speaks. "I like it."

"Me too," I say.

Hippie Chick and Phantom Boy.

We make a pretty good team.

Author's Note

Portland, Oregon, has been my hometown for the past thirty years, so it's only fitting to set Mac's story in this city known for its "weird." Yes, there is an annual World Naked Bike Ride in the city in June, and yes, food carts and cart pods are everywhere. To my knowledge there is no treasure hunt like Mac and Joey participated in, but wouldn't it be fun if there were? Portlanders, please forgive me for the creative liberties I took while writing this book. Many places I mention are real, and some no longer exist (goodbye Alder Street carts). Other places were changed or completely made-up. I take full responsibility for errors in bus lines, street names, and general landscape details. Let's all continue to "Keep Portland Weird."

On a serious note, I want to acknowledge the millions of people who are homeless across our city and nation. How communities decide to tackle this humanitarian issue will

261

remain a great challenge. There are so many compassion-ate, hardworking organizations that are helping, and they are always seeking volunteers. Kids can help too. Donation drives, sack meal programs, hygiene kits, and assisting at food banks or shelters are all possibilities. The best piece of advice I can offer comes from Emily Coleman at Transition Projects in Portland. Emily says, "One of the easiest and most important things (a person) can do to impact the lives of people experiencing homelessness is just to acknowledge them; it can be a tremendously dehumanizing experience, and so many people are in the habit of looking the other way. A simple friendly greeting to our neighbors without homes can go a long way toward helping people feel seen, recognized, and cared for as a human being."

So, make eye contact. Wave. Say hello. Smile.

There's nothing weird about showing compassion.

Acknowledgments

I'll start with a heartfelt thank-you to the incredible team at HarperCollins who assisted me in this exciting journey. Erica Sussman, my extraordinary editor, along with Louisa Currigan, encouraged me and pushed me to make Mac's story stronger, and occasionally weirder. Copy editors Martha Schwartz and Jon Howard, thank you for your concentrated effort to correct my endless comma omissions and my formatting challenges. Tremendous gratitude goes to the jacket design duo of artist Nathan Hackett and designer Jenna Stempel-Lobell. Your attention to detail brought me to tears. To publicist Olivia Russo, I send you a warm thanks for your assistance with author bookings. To the wonderful sales team I had the pleasure of meeting—Kathy Faber, Johanna Schutter, Sabrina Abballe, and Andrea Pappenheimer—thank you all for championing children's literature and getting our books into stores.

Ted Malawer, my awesome agent, I cannot thank you enough for steering me down the publication path (and guiding me at the forks) and for answering my occasional weird questions or referring them to others as needed.

Thank you to my husband, Steve, my loving partner in this life journey. Your support over these last three years has gone above and beyond as I've navigated two full-time jobs. DTHOOY!

Alli and Ryan, you fill my heart with your sibling duets, your joy, and your laughter. My eyes may glaze over when you discuss programming, and calculus, but on the inside, I'm glowing with pride at your intelligence and your work ethic and your desire to succeed. I love you both so much.

Hugs of immense gratitude go to my extended families, the Johnson-Walters-Welker-Lutt clans and the Little-Hansen-Divens-Hall clans. I love all of you. Stay weird.

Every writer needs her writing people, and I found mine years ago and do not plan to let them go. Sandy Grubb, Sarvinder Naberhaus, Suzanne Klein, Jill Van Den Eng, Diana Schaffter, Ann Green, and Kerry McGee, you are all amazing writers. Special thanks to Sandy and Kerry (and her daughter Natalie) for reading early drafts of Mac's story. The Society of Children's Book Writers and Illustrators earns my gratitude as well, particularly the Oregon Region. Thank you for helping children's writers learn, grow, network, celebrate, and plan our futures. To my #Novel19 group, you awe me with your talent. I want to meet every one of you someday.

Teachers need their people too, and I belong to a staff filled with excellence at Jacob Wismer Elementary. Special gratitude goes to my third-grade teammates and support staff from the past five years for their endless patience while I shared my energies between teaching and writing: Patty, Catherine, Barb, Mary D, Kat, Stephanie M, Allison, Annette, Pamela, Hristina, Heidi C, Yvette, Lisa, Amy, Kathy, Charlene, and our super-sub, Susan.

To the hundreds of students I've had the pleasure to work with, you've all made me a better teacher and person. I believe in you. Work hard. Be kind. Go embrace your weird.

There are so many friends in my life from high school, college, and beyond who have supported me long before I became a published author. I treasure your kindness, your camaraderie, and your cheerleading. Special shout-outs to John, Melanie, Kirsten, Sheila, Dave, Heather, Mike, Leslie, and the entire Vo family. And to the most wonderful sister in world, Julie, thank you for being my forever best friend!

To my yoga community at Bikram Freemont Street, you are all beautiful in every way. We may not have goats, but we have plenty of "yoga bliss."

I remain eternally grateful and blessed beyond words.

Cheers to all!